LIT
CA

W. R. BURNETT

NO EXIT PRESS

1989

No Exit Press
18 Coleswood Road
Harpenden, Herts AL5 1EQ

First published in 1929

British Library Cataloguing in Publication Data

Burnett, W. R. (William Riley), 1899–1982
Little Caesar – (No Exit Press Vintage Crime)
I. Title
813′.52[F]

ISBN 0 948353 53 8

9 8 7 6 5 4 3 2 1

Printed by William Collins, Glasgow

To

MARJORIE

The first law of every being, is to preserve itself and live. You sow hemlock, and expect to see ears of corn ripen.

Macchiavelli

NOTE: The characters and events in this book are entirely imaginary.

PART 1

I

Sam Vettori sat staring down into Halsted Street. He was a big man, fat as a hog, with a dark oily complexion, kinky black hair and a fat aquiline face. In repose he had an air of lethargic good-nature, due entirely to his bulk; for in reality he was sullen, bad-tempered and cunning. From time to time he dragged out a huge gold watch and looked at it with raised eyebrows and pursed lips.

Near him at a round table sat Otero, called The Greek, Tony Passa, and Sam Vettori's lieutenant, Rico, playing stud for small stakes. Under the green-shaded lamp Otero's dark face looked livid and cavernous. He sat immobile and said nothing, win or lose. Tony, robust and rosy, scarcely twenty years old, watched each turn of the cards intently, shouting with joy when his luck was good, cursing when it was bad, more out of excitement than interest in the stakes. Rico sat with his hat tilted over his eyes, his pale thin face slightly drawn, his fingers tapping. Rico always played to win.

Vettori, puffing, pulled himself to his feet and began to walk up and down.

"Where you suppose he is?" he asked the ceiling. "I told him eight o'clock. It is half-past."

"Joe never knows what time it is," said Tony.

"Joe's no good," said Rico without taking his eyes off the cards, "he's soft."

"Well," said Vettori, stopping to watch the game out of

boredom, "maybe so. But we can't do without him, Rico. I tell you, Rico, he can go anywhere. A front is what he's got. Swell hotels? What does it mean to that boy? He says to the clerk, I would like please a suite. A suite! You see, Rico. We can't do without him."

Rico tapped on the table, flushing slightly.

"All right, Sam," he said, "some day he'll turn yellow. Hear what I say. He's not right. What's all this dancing? A man don't dance for money."

Sam laughed.

"Oh, Rico! You don't know Joe."

Tony stared at Rico.

"Rico," he said, "Joe's right. I know what I'm saying. All that dancing is a front. He's smart. Have they ever got him once?"

Rico slammed down his cards. He hated Joe and he knew that Tony and Vettori knew it.

"All right," he said, "hear what I say. He'll turn yellow some day. A man don't take money for dancing."

"I win," said Otero.

Rico pushed the money toward him and got to his feet.

"Well, if he don't show up in ten minutes I'll take the air," said Rico.

"You stay where you are," said Vettori, his face hardening.

Tony watched the two of them intently. Otero counted his money. One day Vettori said to Rico, "Rico, you are getting too big for us." Tony remembered the look he had seen in Rico's eyes. Lately they had all been talking about it. Rico was getting too big for them. Scabby, the informer, said: "Tony, mark what I say. It's Rico or Sam. One or the other."

"I'll stay ten minutes," said Rico.

Vettori sat down by the window and stared into Halsted Street.

"Two-fifty," said Otero.

"I'll match you for it," said Tony.

"No," said Otero.

Joe Massara opened the door and came in.

"Well," said Vettori, "you call this eight o'clock?"

Joe got out of a big ulster. He was in evening clothes. His black hair was sleek and parted in the middle. He was vain of his resemblance to the late Mr. Rudolph Valentino.

"Sorry," said Joe, "the bridge was up. Well, what's the dirt?"

"Draw up a chair," said Vettori, "all of you."

They grouped themselves around the table under the green-shaded lamp. Joe put his hands on the table so they could see his well-manicured nails and the diamond ring the dancer, Olga Stassoff, had given him.

"Now," said Vettori, "I'll do the talking. I know what I got to say and you birds keep quiet till I'm through. . . ."

"How long will it take?" asked Joe, smiling.

"Shut up and listen," said Rico.

"All right, all right," said Vettori, patting them both, "no bad blood. Now: ever heard of the Casa Alvarado?"

"Sure," said Joe, "it's an up and up place. One of Francis Wood's joints. I nearly got an engagement there once."

Rico spread out his hands.

"See? They know him. He won't do."

"No, they never seen me. It was all done through an agent."

"All right," said Vettori, "that's the place."

Joe looked startled. Rico smiled and taking off his hat began to comb his hair with a little ivory pocket comb.

"It'd be tough," said Joe, "what's in it?"

"Plenty," said Vettori. "They only bank once or twice a week. They're careless, get that; because they've never been tapped. It's easy."

Joe took out a gold cigarette case which he handled with ostentation.

"Well? I'm listening."

Vettori refused a cigarette and pulled out a stogie. Downstairs a jazzband began to play and a saxophone sent vibrations along the floor.

"Nine o'clock," said Otero.

Vettori lit his stogie.

"They got a safe," he said, "that a baby could crack. Too easy to talk about. But that's on the side. What we're after is the cashier. The place is lousy with jack. I got the lowdown from Scabby. Well, what do you say, Joe?"

"Yeah," Rico cut in, "take it or leave it. We ain't begging you."

Vettori's face hardened but he said nothing.

"If you say it's good," said Joe, "it's good with me."

"All right, all right," said Vettori. "Now, you Tony; we want a big car. Get that. A big, fast car. Get one when I tell you. Steve's got the plates all ready. Yeah?"

"I'm on, Sam."

Tony pulled out a cigarette and lit it with a flourish, but his hands shook a little.

"Rico and Otero," said Vettori, looking at each in turn, "will handle the rods. Yeah?"

Rico said nothing. But Otero smiled, showing his stained teeth, and said:

"That's us, eh, Rico?"

"Well," Vettori went on, "I guess we got that over. Now, Joe, I want you on the inside. Dress yourself up like you are, see, and fix it so you'll get there at midnight. All the whistles'll be tooting and everybody'll be drunk and won't know nothing. See? Now you get there at midnight and go to the cigar counter for change. At twelve-five the fun'll begin. We'll set our watches by telephone, because I don't want you here that night. All right. Rico and Otero come in quick, maybe Tony, too, if you can get a good safe place to park. That's up to Rico. He's bossing the job."

Rico looked at Joe.

"Now, they'll stick you up if everything's O.K. If not, give them the high sign and they'll beat it. We ain't taking no chances, because one night don't make much difference, only New Year's Eve's a good night, see? All right. You play like you don't know them, got it? But while they're working, you got your eyes open, see? And if something happens, you got a rod, but don't use it. We got to watch that."

Vettori shifted his stogie and shook his finger sideways at Rico.

"That's your trouble, Rico. The Big Boy can't fix murder. He can fix anything but murder. Get that. You're too quick with the lead. If that guy over at the pool room'd died we wouldn't none of us be sitting here right now. . . ."

Otero broke in vehemently, surprising them.

"But he had to! He had to! Rico does what is right."

"All right," said Vettori, "but take it easy. Now, Joe, you

got your hands up, but you watch. If nothing happens nobody knows the difference. But if something does happen you pull the rod and help the boys get out. All right. Here's the dope. Get what's in the cash register first. Get that because that's easy. If things go right, tackle the safe; it'll probably be open. Another thing: no frisking in the lobby. That's too dangerous and takes too long. Let the yaps keep their money. All right."

Vettori took a map from his pocket and spread it out on the table. The men crowded round him.

"You go straight in," said Vettori, marking the route with a pencil, "on the right is the check-room; watch the girls behind the counter, Joe. On the left is the cigar counter and the cashier's desk. At the end of the lobby is a big door; the real joint's beyond that. If things go right, nobody in the place'll know it's been stuck up, except maybe some yaps in the lobby. Get the idea? With all them horns tooting and all that damn noise, see? All right. On the right of the lobby is a door and that goes into the manager's office. The box is in there. The manager's a goddamn bohunk and there ain't an ounce of fight in him. See? Scabby give me the lowdown."

Vettori rolled up his map, put it in his pocket, then looked at his watch.

"Well," he said, "got it all?"

Joe turned his diamond ring round on his finger and looked at the table.

"What's the word, Joe?" said Rico.

"It's a tough one, Rico. What's the guarantee?"

"Guarantee, hell!" cried Rico. "Why, a blind guy could do your stand."

"Well, I ain't doing no time for fifty bucks," said Joe.

Vettori laughed.

"I'll give you a couple hundred now," he said.

Joe nodded.

"All right. I'm in. Never mind the couple hundred."

They all got to their feet. Below them the jazzband was still playing and the saxophone was still sending vibrations along the floor.

"What'll you have, boys," said Vettori, "want some drinks sent up?"

"Not me," said Tony, "I'm going over and see my woman."

Otero clapped his hands.

"He's got a woman."

Rico hit Otero on the back.

"The Greek's got a woman too," said Rico.

Otero with his hands cupped made a series of curves in the air. Joe was patronizing; Olga Stassoff, the dancer, was his woman.

"A beauty is shë, Otero?"

"Si, señor."

"Well," said Vettori, "want any drinks sent up?"

"Sure," said Joe, "send me up a snort. I guess Rico'll take milk."

Rico didn't drink.

"All right about Rico," said Vettori in a good humour, "he's a smart boy."

Tony went out followed by Vettori.

"I think I go see my woman," said Otero.

Joe laughed. Rico said :

"Goodbye, Otero. Give Seal Skin a rub for me."

When Otero had gone, Joe said :

"Has old Seal Skin got The Greek hooked yet?"

"Well," said Rico, "he spends a lot of jack on her. She ain't much to look at and she's pretty old, but what's the difference?"

Joe never could figure Rico out. Women didn't seem to interest him.

Rico went over to the window and stood looking out at the electric sign on a level with his eyes.

CLUB
P
A
L
E
R
M
O
DANCING

Rico and Joe felt queer alone together. They were silent. Joe took out his gold cigarette case and lit a cigarette. Snow began to fall past the window.

"Look," said Rico, "it's snowing."

"Yeah," said Joe, looking up mechanically, "snowing hard."

2

VETTORI was sitting in his little office on the main floor. On the other side of the wall the jazzband was playing, but he paid no attention. The noise of the jazzband was the same to him as the ticking of a clock to an ordinary person. He felt very pleasant and comfortable over his bottle of wine and his plate of spaghetti. Things were right!

He congratulated himself on his subordinates. Each man a specialist. Yes, yes! That was the way to do. None of this hit or miss stuff for Sam Vettori. Rico the best gunman in Little Italy; a swelled head, all right, but he can be handled, and there you are! Otero so crazy about Rico he "don't know nothing". Follow Rico any place; do anything Rico tells him. And handy with a rod. Well, well. Not bad for a Mexican. As a rule foreigners were not right with Sam Vettori, but in general he had an open mind, and Otero was the goods. And look at Joe Massara, there was a man for you! A swell Italian who could pass anywhere. One winter in Florida, so they say, Joe passed himself off as a count and hooked a rich widow for plenty. Yes, yes! That was Joe for you. As an inside man you couldn't beat him. And Tony! He could drive a car sixty miles an hour straight up the Tribune Tower. Only one thing, sometimes Tony was undependable. Used to be a choir boy at St. Dominick's and that stuff. But he had outgrown that, maybe; anyway he was dead scared of Rico and that would shut his mouth.

Vettori leaned back, wiped his mouth with the back of his hand and unbuttoned his vest. Spaghetti and wine, what is better!

The band stopped playing. Bat Carillo, the bouncer, put his head in the door.

"Couple of hard guys looking for trouble, boss," he said.

Vettori looked up.

"Yeah? Know them?"

"Never seen them before."

Vettori heaved himself to his feet and walked with Carillo to the swinging doors which separated the back-rooms and kitchen from the club proper. He pushed the door open about a foot and peered in. Carillo pointed.

Vettori laughed and closed the door.

"Some of them dumb Irish," he said; "let 'em alone unless they get bad and start something, then bounce 'em."

"O.K., boss," said Carillo.

Waiters passed Vettori in the corridor, sweat dropping from their faces, steam rising from the dishes on the slanted trays. Vettori rubbed his hands.

"Business is good. Well, well! We won't none of us die in the poor house."

When he got back to his office he found Scabby, the informer, waiting for him. Scabby was dark and undersized with a heavy, sullen, blotched face. Passing as a police informer, he was in reality a member of the Vettori gang. He played a dangerous game as he informed on other gangs. His life wasn't worth a cent and he was jumpy and quick with a gun.

"Well, well, Giovanni," said Vettori, "what's the news?"

"Everything's jake," said Scabby, taking off his hat and revealing a shining bald head.

Vettori called a waiter.

"Some spaghetti for this man here," he said, "and a bottle of wine."

"That's the ticket," said Scabby without smiling; he never smiled; his face was melancholy and lined, and sagged like a hound's. "The boys on?"

"All set," said Vettori. "It looks easy."

Scabby nodded.

"It ought to be. But no gunplay, get that, Sam. The Big Boy'd raise hell if he knew what was up."

Vettori's face hardened.

"I heard that once, Scabby. That's enough. This is too good to pass up."

"All right," said Scabby, "I've had my say. But things ain't what they used to be, Sam. It's getting dangerous. They've even got the Big Boy scared. It's the damn newspapers. They play that crime stuff off the boards. Big headlines, see? That's the trouble."

They sat silent. Vettori, absorbed, puffed on his stogie. Finally he said :

"Listen, Scabby, you ain't heard nothing, see? I got to keep these boys on their toes. Especially Joe. Don't spill nothing about the Big Boy."

Scabby shook his head vigorously. Vettori took out his bill-fold and handed Scabby a fifty.

"That's part of your split, Scabby. Keep your eyes open, that's all."

Scabby pocketed the money. The waiter came in bringing the spaghetti and the wine. Carillo put his head in the door.

"Reilly, the dick's, up front."

Vettori nodded.

"He's O.K. If he sticks around, send him back in about half an hour."

"Sure," said Scabby, "I'll be out of here in less than that."

3

OTERO lay looking out the window at the electric sign across the street.

CLUB
P
A
L
E
R
M
O
DANCING

Snow was falling past the windows. Otero lay smoking a big twenty-five cent cigar and singing softly to himself. He always sang when he was with Seal Skin.

"Some snow," said Otero.

"Yeah, some snow," said Seal Skin, who was sitting with her feet on the window sill, smoking one of Otero's cigar.

"Heavy like cotton," said Otero.

"Yeah," said Seal Skin.

"Where I used to be it never snowed."

"Didn't it?"

"No, it never snowed."

Seal Skin blew out a cloud of smoke.

"How come you ever left Mexico, Ramón?"

"Well, I don't know." Otero scratched his head. "I just left."

"Was they after you?"

"No, I just left."

Otero got up and put his arms around Seal Skin.

"Some girl," he said.

Seal Skin gave him a push.

"Wait'll I finish this."

"Sure, sure," said Otero, smiling and patting her on the shoulder.

"Look," said Seal Skin, "you're a good guy, Ramón. But dumb. How come you hang after Rico?"

"Rico is a great man."

Seal Skin laughed out loud.

"Yeah? Great, but careless. He'll never die of old age."

Otero didn't understand.

"What you say?"

"They'll fill him full of lead. He's too cocky."

Otero shook his head.

"No, they'll never get Rico."

"They get 'em all."

"No," said Otero, "they'll never get Rico. Once I say to him, 'Look, you must be careful.' But he say, 'Not me, they'll never get Rico.' "

Seal Skin opened the window and flung her cigar down into the street. A gust of cold air rushed into the overheated room.

"Listen," she said, "that's bunk. Rico's no different from

anybody else. You stick with Rico long enough and you'll have a swell funeral. Why don't you get into the beer racket? That's safe."

"I go with Rico," said Otero. "What do I care? I have no people. Once I had a brother but they shot him."

"The cops?"

"No, the rurales. He was with Villa."

"Who the hell's Villa?"

"Villa was a great man, like Rico."

Seal Skin got up and took a drink from a bottle on the bureau. Then she said:

"Let's hit the hay, Ramón."

"Sure, sure," said Otero.

4

It was nearly two o'clock when Tony left his woman. A lake wind was blowing hard and the snow fell heavily past the street lights. Tony muffled himself in his overcoat and pulled his cap low. He felt tired and disgusted.

At the corner near his home, he turned into Sicily Pete's restaurant. Three Italians were playing cards at a table in the back. Up front a mechanical piano ground out The Rosary.

"Hello, Tony, how's the boy?" said Pete.

"Not so good," said Tony.

"You ain't looking any too good, Tony," said Pete.

Tony ran his hands over his face and stared at his image in the mirror behind the counter. Pale; circles under his eyes.

"Well, I guess I'll live," said Tony.

Pete smacked the counter with both hands.

"Love of God! Sure you'll live. You be O.K. tomorrow morning. I know, Tony, my boy. Don't forget I was a young fellow once. I know. I know."

"Sure you know," said Tony, sarcastic.

"Sure I do. You think I don't know about that little red head. Hot stuff, Tony, my boy. Only don't be a fool. Save some for tomorrow night."

Pete laughed shaking all over and smacked the counter with his hands.

"What the hell's wrong with you, Pete?" cried one of the card players.

"Never you mind. All right, Tony, what'll you have?"

Tony couldn't decide. Pete went to wait on one of the card players. The mechanical piano finished The Rosary on a discord. Tony went over and put a nickel in the slot.

"I got a combination to go and two Javas," cried Pete.

The mechanical piano began to play O Sole Mio.

"I'll take a combination," said Tony, "and a cup of Java."

"O.K.," said Pete; "I got two combinations, one to go and three on the Java."

"How's business, Pete?" asked Tony.

"Oh, what you call so-so. Not good, not bad. I never get rich here."

"Why don't you put in a line of bottled goods?" said Tony, smiling.

Pete raised both hands over his head and brought them down hard on the counter.

"None of that for Sicily Pete. Oh no. Pete's too smart for that. If the bulls don't get you, why, some of them gangsters do. I know. One say, you buy from me; the other say, no, you buy from me. All the same. No matter who you buy from, bango!"

Pete brought Tony his combination and his coffee and stood at the counter with him while he ate it.

"Tony," said Pete, putting his head on one side, "you know you look like your old man. Other day when you was in here I say to the missus, look, ain't he just like his old man? Well, well. That is good. A boy should look like his old man. That is a good sign."

"Knew the old man pretty well, didn't you, Pete?" said Tony, finishing his coffee.

"Yes, pretty well. When he was a young fellow he was like you. Full of pep and always after the girls. But I don't know, your mama she got hold of him, then he wasn't like he used to be. He wasn't like the same fellow. Pretty soon he died."

Tony laughed.

"Hard on the old lady, ain't you?"

"Love of God, no," said Pete, an expression of acute misery on his face, "you don't get me, Tony. I mean he got to be a good fellow, like me. Work, work, that's all he knew. Well, work is a good thing. It keeps you out of trouble, but I don't know..."

Pete wiped the sweat from his forehead and meditated. Tony flipped him a fifty-cent piece. The mechanical piano stopped on a prolonged, slurred discord.

"Well, I guess I'll hit for home," said Tony, "so long, Pete."

"Good night, Tony," said Pete with one of his blandest smiles, "come in again."

The wind struck Tony in the face as he left the restaurant. The streets were white and silent. Tony walked home slowly, tired and disgusted.

As he entered the flat he saw a dim light in the front room. He tried to sneak into his bedroom, but his mother heard him. She rose from her chair, a monstrous silhouette against the dim front room light.

"A fine time for you to come in, Antonio," she said. "Have you been out again with them good-for-nothing loafers?"

"Yes," said Tony, in a bad temper.

"So . . . !" said his mother, "you don't even lie any more. Well, well! You are doing fine. Pretty soon you won't come home at all, you bum."

"You said a mouthful," said Tony.

"Sure, you won't listen to your mother. Some day you'll remember what I told you. You loaf with crooks and bums long enough, you'll see what will happen."

"All right," said Tony, going into his room and banging the door behind him.

His mother stood in the middle of the room for a minute, then she put out the light and sat in the dark, crying.

5

The little blonde check-girl helped Joe take off his big ulster, her hand lingering on his arm. He handed her a quarter.

"Don't go on a bat with that two-bits," he said.

"No, sir," said the check-girl.

She watched him walk across the long dance floor, pick his way among the crowded tables, bowing from time to time to one he had jostled, and disappear through the employees' door at the back. Then she put checks on his coat and hat and hung them up.

"God, what a hot-looking man," she said; "I don't see how that little hunky got him."

Olga Stassoff was just putting the finishing touches to her make-up. Joe came in softly and stood watching her. She began to sing.

"If you're singing for me," said Joe, "you can stop any time."

Olga turned around.

"Well, what are you doing here? Broke?"

"Shut up," said Joe.

Then he turned and walked out of the room. Olga jumped to her feet and ran after him. She caught him near the employees' door. He pushed her away.

"Ain't that a fine way to say hello to a guy!" he said. "Why, you must think you got me roped and hog-tied."

"I was just kidding, Joe," said Olga, "honest I didn't mean it. I was just kidding."

"Well, get this," said Joe, "I'm goddamn sick of that line. What do you take me for? That goes big with some of your swell boy friends who've got ugly wives and ain't any too particular, but me! I don't take that kind of talk from nobody."

Olga put her arms around him, but he pushed her away.

"Listen, Joe," she said, "I got good news for you, so get out of your fighting clothes and come to earth. Can't you take a little kidding?"

Joe took out his gold cigarette case and selected a cigarette. He always smoked the best, when Olga had plenty of money, and he usually carried three or four different brands. With a flourish he put away his case, then, very preoccupied, he placed the selected cigarette on the back of his left hand and, with a slight tap of his right hand, flipped it into his mouth. Olga laughed.

"Now," said Joe, "spill the good news."

DeVoss, the manager, came through the swinging doors.
"Have you told him yet, Olga?" he asked.
Joe gave the manager a most ingratiating smile.
"What's the big talk, Mr. DeVoss? Am I missing something?"
"You sure are," said DeVoss. "The Stranskys broke their contract and I'm putting you on in their place."
Joe leapt into the air and executed a twinkle. Olga burst out laughing.
"Well," said Joe, "how much?"
"One hundred to start, Joe, then we'll see."
"Well," said Joe, "I can't buy no limousines with that, but I'll take it."
Joe and DeVoss shook hands.
"Now," said the manager, "there's a girl out here who's just dying to dance with you, Joe."
Joe shook his head.
"No, I don't like that stuff. They always think they got to hand you something. What the hell! I don't want no dame handing me nothing."
Olga put her hand over her mouth.
"Don't worry about that, Joe," said DeVoss, "she already asked me about that and I told her you'd be insulted so she gave me a ten." DeVoss took a crumpled bill out of his pocket and handed it to Joe. "There, now get this. She's an up and up girl and she means lots of business to this place. Her old man's got a couple of million bucks and she's the real thing. All right, Joe?"
"Sure, sure," said Joe, "always willing to oblige."
DeVoss went through the swinging doors and stood waiting for Joe on the other side. Olga took Joe by the arm.
"Listen," she said, "none of your funny business now. Just do your stuff and leave it at that. I'm on to these society women. I know what they want."
Joe leapt into the air and executed another twinkle.
"Alley up!" he cried, "don't you trust me, baby?"
Olga put her hands on her hips and began to laugh. How could you be sore at a guy like that?

6

Rico was standing in front of his mirror, combing his hair with a little ivory pocket comb. Rico was vain of his hair. It was black and lustrous, combed straight back from his low forehead and arranged in three symmetrical waves.

Rico was a simple man. He loved but three things: himself, his hair and his gun. He took excellent care of all three.

PART 2

I

"HEAR me," said Rico, his face twitching, "he's turned yellow. He's turned yellow. What the hell you expect from a choir boy!"

Otero said nothing but sat with his chair tipped back against the wall smoking a cigarette, his eyes closed. Sam Vettori stood in the middle of the room and stared at his watch.

"Keep your shirt on, Rico," said Vettori, "you're on edge."

"Sure, Rico," said Otero.

Carillo came in without knocking. Vettori put away his watch.

"Well!"

"O.K., boss," said Carillo, "Tony's in the alley."

Vettori took out his watch again.

"Rico, it's eleven-thirty-five. What do you say?"

"Let's get going."

Otero got slowly to his feet, stamped out his cigarette, and, taking the riot gun from the table in front of him, slipped it under his overcoat. Rico examined his big automatic.

Carillo went out, softly closing the door. Otero walked over and patted Rico on the shoulder.

"O.K., now, eh, Rico?"

Rico smiled. Vettori's face was covered with sweat and

he pulled out a big white silk handkerchief to mop it.

"Rico," he said, "from now on you boss the job. Only, get this : for the love of God, no gunwork. That's all. I ain't ripe for the rope."

Rico said nothing. Otero shrugged.

Vettori, still mopping his face, opened a window and a gust of cold air rushed in.

Rico took out his little ivory pocket comb and mechanically combed his hair. Then he put on his hat and tilted it over his eyes.

"Well," he said to Otero, "let's go."

Otero followed Rico out. Vettori called :

"Make it clean, Rico. Make it clean."

They went down the back stairs. Carillo was waiting at the foot of the stairs and held the alley door open for them. The alley-way was dark and Otero stumbled.

"Caramba !"

"Watch that gun," said Rico.

Tony was sitting at the wheel of a big, open Cadillac. He tossed his cigarette away and said :

"Well, here we are."

Rico said nothing, but got into the front seat with Tony. Otero got into the back seat. Carillo stood looking at them for a moment, then closed the door. Tony stepped on the starter.

"All right," said Rico, "let's go, but take it easy. We got lots of time."

They took it easy. Tony drove along as leisurely as though they were going to a New Year's party. Rico leaned back and smoked, watching all the passing cars. Otero, who had removed the riot gun and had it on the seat beside him, was sitting bolt upright, his hands on his knees. He could never get used to riding in an automobile. Rico turned and saw the gun.

"Put that rod on the floor," he said.

Otero obeyed.

It had got colder. The snow was no longer falling and a chilly wind was blowing up in gusts from the lake. The streets were nearly deserted. Over west a whistle began to blow, discordant and shrill.

"Well," said Tony, nodding in the direction of the whistle, "it won't be long now."

But Rico leaned over and hissed in his ear.

"Police car!"

A big Packard with a hooded machine-gun in the back seat passed them. There were two plain-clothes men in the front and two in the back.

"What'll I do?" asked Tony.

One of the men leaned out and stared back at them.

"Jesus," said Tony, "he's looking at us."

"Keep your shirt on," said Rico, putting his hand on Tony's arm.

Otero took a cigarette from his pack and rolled it between his palms.

The police car slowed up. Rico's fingers closed on Tony's arm.

"Here's an alley," said Rico, "duck!"

Tony took the turn on two wheels, just missing a parked car. Otero was thrown from one end of his seat to the other, losing his cigarette. The Cadillac's exhaust roared in the narrow alley-way. There was nothing but darkness ahead of them.

"It's a blind," said Tony.

"No," said Rico, "I know this place like a book. Turn to your right at the end."

Rico leaned out and stared back. Then he laughed.

"Ain't that like the damn dummies! Nothing in sight."

They came back to Michigan Boulevard by a wide detour. Here the wind blew fiercely, raising little whirlwinds of snow. Now there were whistles blowing in all parts of town. Rico looked at his wrist watch.

"Five of twelve. All right, Tony. Step on it."

"What time, Rico?" asked Otero.

Rico told him.

"Fine, fine," said Otero, "eh, Rico?"

Half a block down the street they saw the huge electric sign of the Casa Alvarado. The street was deserted except for the parked cars. They drove along slowly now.

Rico leaned out.

"That's a break," he said, pointing to a parking place where they couldn't be hemmed in. "Listen, Tony, this ain't going to be no cinch, so you better give us a lift."

Tony pretended to be preoccupied with parking.

"Get me?"

Tony was pale and his lips were twitching.

"That ain't my stand, Rico," he said.

Rico looked at him. Tony sat silent for a moment, then, pulling at the vizer of his cap, said:

"But you're the boss, Rico."

"O.K.," said Rico, smiling. "Now, Otero, get this. I go first. You follow me with the big rod. I stick up the cashier. Tony swings the sacks. Got it?" Rico took three small neatly-folded canvas sacks out of his pocket and handed them to Tony. "Otero, you watch the door. If you see anybody coming in, let 'em come in, then back 'em up against the wall. If things go right, I'll tap the box. Got it?"

Rico looked at his watch. It was three minutes past twelve.

"Let's go," he said.

Otero got out lazily, hiding the riot gun under his coat. Rico got out, followed by Tony.

"Got your rod, Tony?" asked Rico.

Tony nodded.

"All right, keep it in your pocket. Maybe you won't need it right away. If anybody gets funny, why, pull it."

"O.K.," said Tony, "but for God's sake, Rico, no gunwork."

Otero said:

"You leave Rico alone. He does what is right."

Whistles were blowing all over town. They walked up the carpet which was laid across the pavement under the canvas marquee. Inside there was a blaze of lights and they could hear the music. The lobby was deserted except for two checkgirls, one waiter, a cigar clerk, and the cashier, a pale woman with a green eyeshade, who was perched on a stool. Joe Massara, in a big ulster and a derby hat, was standing at the cigar counter, kidding the clerk. He saw them out of the corner of his eye and nodded twice.

They came in quickly, Rico in front with his big automatic at ready, Otero slightly behind him and to the left, carrying the sawed-off shotgun hip-high, Tony in the rear, his hand in his overcoat pocket.

Before Rico could say anything, Joe Massara faced them, put his back up against the counter and raised his hands.

"My God," he cried, "it's a hold-up."

One of the check-girls screamed piercingly. The waiter's knees buckled and he almost fell. The others stood petrified.

"You're goddamn right it's a hold-up!" shouted Rico, trying to intimidate them, "and it ain't gonna be no picnic. Get that, all of you birds. I got lead in this here rod and my finger's itching. One crack out of any of you and they'll pat you with a spade. All right, Tony."

Tony, white as chalk, took the sacks out of his pocket and walked over to the cashier's desk. The cashier was standing behind the register, hands raised. When Tony came up she said:

"Take anything you want, only for God's sake don't touch me."

"O.K.," said Tony, "clean out the box but don't get funny."

Tony held the sacks while the cashier scooped the money into them. Tony saw pack after pack of wrapped greenbacks drop into the sacks. He began to feel a little better.

Rico left the cashier to Tony, but looked at each of the others in turn, his eyes, under his tilted hat, intimidating them as successfully as the big Luger in his hand. Otero stood behind him and a little to the left, impassive, the riot gun hip-high.

The manager opened the door of his office and with a dazed look hesitated for a moment, then, with a great sigh, put his back against the wall and raised his hands. He was a Czech with a swarthy complexion which gradually turned greenish.

Rico glared at the manager.

"Stay put you!" he said.

"All right, all right," said the Czech.

Joe Massara said:

"Jesus, my arm's paralyzed."

"Yeah," shouted Rico, "well, don't let it drop."

"All set," cried Tony.

Otero was busy at the door with a man in a top hat who had just come in. The man couldn't believe his eyes and kept muttering:

"Good Lord! Good Lord!"

Otero backed him against the wall.

In the club proper, beyond the big arched doorways, the band was playing loudly, horns were tooting, people were shouting.

"All right," said Rico, "get out your gat, Tony. I'll tap the box inside."

"God," said Tony, "it'll take too long."

Rico looked at him. Tony, holding the sacks in one arm, pulled out his gun. Rico walked over to the manager.

"Listen," he said, "I want action. Go in and open that box and slip me the jack. One funny move and I'll blow your guts out."

"Oh, my God!" cried the Czech.

They disappeared. There was a dead silence in the lobby. One of the check-girls began to cry.

"Nice little hold-up," said Joe.

Nobody said anything.

"Yeah," said Joe, nonchalant, "fine little hold-up."

He smiled at the waiter, who looked hastily away and turned agonized eyes on Tony as if to say: "Look, I can't help what that bird's saying."

Two more men came in the street door and were backed up against the wall by Otero. The seconds seemed like hours to Tony, who was slowly losing his nerve.

The manager reappeared, followed by Rico, who had his gun pressed against the manager's back. Rico's pockets bulged.

"Good Lord," hissed Tony, "let's go."

Three men and two women came out into the lobby from the club proper. They stopped, petrified.

The strain was beginning to tell on Rico, whose face was ghastly.

"Stick up your hands, you," he cried, "and don't move."

Two of the men and both of the women put up their hands, but the third man, burly and red-faced, hesitated.

"Good God," said Joe, "it's Courtney, the bull."

Joe's mask of nonchalance slipped from him instantly; he dropped his hands and reached for his gun.

"Beat it," cried Rico to Tony and Otero.

They made a break for the door. One of the women with Courtney fainted and fell hard, hitting her head.

"Don't touch her," cried Rico, "my finger's itching."

Joe followed the others, backing out with his gun in his hand.

Courtney's face was purple. He glanced at his wife, lying pale and unconscious on the floor, then, shouting "You dirty bums" reached for his gun. Rico fired. Courtney took two steps toward Rico, staring. Then he fell heavily, his arms spread.

At the door Rico collided with a drunken man, who was just entering. The man tried to hug him, but he knocked him down with a blow of his fist.

Rico jumped on the running-board and bellowed:

"Open her up, Tony. This ain't no picnic."

Tony was unnerved and tears were dripping down onto his hands. Joe and Otero sat silent in the back seat. Otero rolled a cigarette between his palms. Nobody said anything.

Tony took a corner, careening. The wind had died down a little and it had begun to snow again, a thin, cold, powdery snow. The whistles were still blowing, but fainter now, one leaving off, then another.

"Well," said Rico, "I plugged him."

"Yeah," said Joe, "I seen him fall. Like a ton of bricks."

"Well," said Otero, "what can you do? The fool, pulling a gat!"

Tony said nothing, but sat with his eyes fixed.

"It's our hips for this," said Joe.

Otero shrugged and lit a cigarette.

"Losing your guts, Joe?" asked Rico.

"Me!" said Joe.

Tony turned into the alley way back of The Palermo. Rico put the sacks under his coat and jumped out. Otero and Joe followed him.

"Tony," said Rico, "ditch that can, then come back for your split. Hear what I say. Ditch it good and proper. We'll wait."

"Look," said Joe, "I got to have my split now. I'm on at one-twenty. Boy, I can't miss that turn."

"O.K.," said Rico.

Tony drove off down the alley. Rico knocked at the door and Carillo let them in.

2

WHEN they came in Vettori was standing in the middle of the room mopping his forehead with his big white silk handkerchief. Beads of sweat stood out all over his swarthy, fat face.

Rico threw the sacks on the table and began to empty his pockets.

"There's the dough," said Rico, "looks like a good haul."

Joe sat down at the table under the green-shaded lamp without taking off his hat or coat. Otero took the riot gun from under his coat and locked it up in a cupboard. Vettori knew there was something the matter. His eyes narrowed.

"Well," he said again.

"Everything was O.K.," said Rico, "only I had to plug a guy."

Vettori fell down into a chair and stared out the window.

"Yeah," said Joe, trying to smile, "and the guy was Courtney."

Vettori put his head on the back of his chair and stared at the ceiling. Then he sat up suddenly and banged on the table with both fists.

"Goddamn!" he cried, "what did I tell you, Rico! What did I tell you! Love of God, didn't I tell you no gunwork?"

Rico was white with rage.

"Listen, Sam, you think I'm gonna let a guy pull a gat on me. What the hell! Any more of them cracks and this is my last job."

Vettori made an elaborate, tragic gesture.

"Yeah, you bet this is your last job."

Joe took off his derby and put it beside him on the table. His face was dead white.

"You said it," said Joe, "they'll get us sure for this."

Vettori shook his big head slowly from side to side.

"They'll get us dead sure for this."

Rico began to comb his hair.

"Maybe you better go over and give yourself up," he said; then dropping his sarcastic tone, "listen, how the hell they gonna get us? Why, you're the finest bunch of yellow bastards I ever seen."

"Not me," said Otero.

Joe tried to smile.

"Wait till you see the papers."

Rico came over and leaned on the table.

"Listen, don't they always play that stuff up in the papers. Courtney's the only guy in the place that ever seen one of us before. Come on, snap out of it. And split the dough."

But Vettori sat inert, mopping his face. Suddenly he asked:

"Where's Tony?"

"He's ditching the can," said Rico.

"Suppose they pick him up?"

Rico began to open the sacks.

"That'll be just too bad," said Joe.

Rico laughed.

"A fine bunch of yeggs!"

Vettori got to his feet in a fury.

"You, Rico! Shut your mouth. You think I want to hang because you get yellow and shoot somebody."

Rico, very calm, put his hand in his pocket and said:

"Sam, you get funny with me and you won't get no split at all. Only a horseshoe wreath."

"Oh, hell, Sam," said Joe, "we're all in it, ain't we? Come on, split the dough."

Vettori sat down. Otero stood a little behind him, watching.

"Since you want it, Sam," said Rico, his face pale and drawn, "you're gonna get it. Listen, you split even, that's all. Hear me! You get an even split."

Vettori said nothing. Joe sat rigid, ready to dive under the table. For months Scabby had been predicting this break; now it had come. Joe feared Vettori and Rico equally, but something told him that Rico would win.

Vettori let his hands fall on the table.

"All right, Rico," he said, "I split even. Sit down and we'll divvy."

But Rico didn't move.

"You got a gun on you, Sam?" he asked.

Vettori looked up at him.

"Sure I got a gun on me."

"Well, don't try to use it."

"No," said Otero, "don't try to use it."

Vettori's face went slack. He sat tapping on the table with his fat fingers.

"Rico," he said, finally, "I split even on the square."

Rico's victory was complete. Joe looked at him with admiration. Sam was a tough bird, but Rico was tougher.

Vettori got up, walked across the room and stood looking out the window.

3

JOE handed Rico a sheet of paper full of figures. Rico read: 9331·75·

"All right," said Rico, "split it five ways and we'll make up Scabby's split between us."

Otero sat with his chair tipped back against the wall, smoking a cigarette with his eyes closed. Vettori was playing solitaire and swearing softly to himself.

Joe looked at his watch.

"Quarter till. I got to beat it. Say, Sam, call Carillo and let him get me a cab, will you?"

Sam heaved himself to his feet and called Carillo. In a moment the bouncer put his flattened face in the door.

"Three dicks downstairs, boss?"

"Who are they?" asked Vettori.

"Flaherty and two guys I don't know, boss. They want to see you."

Vettori stood looking at the floor. Carillo jumped in and shut the door.

"Christ," he said, "they're coming up."

Rico leapt to his feet, ran across the room and opened a panel in the wall.

"Come on, Joe," he said, "you can slip out the back way. Stay where you are, Otero, and go right on smoking. Send Joe's cab around in the alley, Bat."

Vettori looked at Rico.

"You suppose they know something, Rico?"

"Not unless they picked Tony up. You don't know nothing, Sam, see? I'll be right here listening, and if there's any trouble, why, it'll be tough on the dicks."

Vettori scooped up the money, wrapped his coat around it, and handed it to Rico. Joe went through the panel, followed by Rico. There was a knock at the door.

Vettori nodded and Carillo opened the door. Two plain-clothes men stepped in and stood looking around the room. One was tall and burly in a huge ulster; the other was short and very young. They both had their right hands in their overcoat pockets.

"All right, Carillo," said Vettori, "go ahead. That's all."

"Wait a minute," said the burly one, "tell Flaherty we'll be down in a couple of minutes, for him to wait."

"Sure, sure," said Carillo.

He went out closing the door softly.

"Well," said Vettori, "you want to see me?"

"Yeah," said the burly one, who did all the talking, "we want to see you, Vettori."

"Well, here I am!"

Otero opened his eyes long enough to look at them, then closed them again and went on smoking.

"Vettori," said the detective, "we want some information."

"Well?"

Vettori sat down at the table and began to shuffle the cards.

"There's a big Cadillac draped around a pole a couple of blocks down the street and we just wondered if you knew anything about it."

Vettori began to lay out a game of solitaire.

"How should I know anything about it? Ain't it got no licence plates on it?"

"Sure, but they're phoney."

"Yeah?"

"Yeah. It was stolen about eight o'clock tonight on the North Side and we got a pretty good description of the guy that stole it."

"Well," said Vettori. "I got a good business. What the hell'd I be doing stealing automobiles."

He laughed and shook his head.

"Oh, you got me wrong," said the detective with elaborate innocence. "You see, it's piled up right straight down the street from here and I thought maybe it was some of the guys from your joint, see? I mean some of the young guys that come here to dance."

"Well," said Vettori, "how would I know?"

The detective took out a cigar and began to chew on it.

"Wasn't there nobody in it?" asked Otero.

"Yeah," said the detective, "one guy. But he beat it."

"I don't know nothing about it," said Vettori.

"Well, no harm in asking," said the detective. "Come on, Mike, let's get going. I guess Vettori don't know nothing about it."

The two of them walked slowly to the door. The big one turned.

"Say, Vettori," he said, "did you hear the news?"

Vettori looked up.

"What news?"

"Why, some bastard bumped Cap Courtney off over at the Casa Alvarado."

"Yeah?" said Vettori, "some guys are sure careless with the lead. That's a tough break."

The young detective opened the door and they started out.

"Ain't it?" said the big one. "Well, so long."

As soon as the door closed, Vettori went over and shot the bolt, then peeped out through the shutter. Rico came out of his hiding place.

"Well," said Vettori, glancing at Rico, "things ain't going so good."

Rico shrugged.

"They don't know nothing. Just feeling around. Listen, Sam, where's your guts? We got to stick together on this."

"I know," said Vettori, falling back into his chair, "but I never seen things break so tough."

Rico held out a roll of bills.

"Here's your split, Sam."

Vettori took the bills and stuffed them into his pocket. Rico handed Otero his. Otero got up and put on his overcoat.

"I think I go see my woman," he said.

When he had gone Rico went over and sat down beside Vettori.

"Listen, Sam," he said, "I been taking orders too long. We're done. Get the idea? But we got to see this through. We get a break and we'll come clean. Only we got to shoot straight. See what I mean? I got a rope around my neck right now and they can only hang you once. If anybody gets yellow and squeals, my gun's gonna speak its piece."

"That's O.K. with me," said Sam.

They sat silent. Downstairs the jazzband was playing and the saxophone was sending vibrations along the floor. Vettori laid out another game of solitaire.

"Funny for Tony to crash," he said.

"He lost his nerve," said Rico.

"You suppose he'll show?"

"Not till tomorrow if he's got any sense. I'll leave his split with you."

4

Rico went over to see Ma Magdalena, the fence. Her fruit store was still open and her son Arrigo was sitting half-asleep beside a pile of oranges.

"Hello," he said.

"Where's Ma?" asked Rico.

Arrigo pulled a cord which rang a bell in the rooms beyond the store. Ma, leaning on her stick, came out into the store. Seeing Rico, she said:

"Oh, it's you! Well, well! Come back. Come back."

"Can I come too, Ma?" said Arrigo.

"You stay and mind the store, you lazy loafer," said Ma, shaking her stick at him.

Arrigo sat down once more by the pile of oranges.

Rico followed Ma Magdalena back into her little office. She pulled up a chair for him and he sat down, then she got out a bottle.

"You talk, I drink," she said, sitting down beside him and pouring herself a drink.

Rico took out his split, peeled off a few bills and handed her the rest.

"Plant it," he said.

She took the roll, counted it, and put it down inside her dress.

"Had a big New Year's Eve, did you?"

"Yeah," said Rico, "plenty big. There'll be lots of fun tomorrow."

"Well, well," said Ma, "that's the way it goes."

She poured herself another glass of wine, then she reached over and touched Rico with her stick.

"Look, Rico, you ain't got a nice little girl who wants a big diamond ring, have you?"

"Me, buy a diamond ring for a skirt?"

Ma Magdalena made a clucking noise and shook her head.

"You are cold, Rico. Don't like wine. Don't like women. You are no good, Rico."

Rico smiled.

"Me, I like women once in a while, but I ain't putting out no diamond rings."

Leaving Ma Magdalena's Rico went in the direction of Sicily Pete's. The wind was blowing hard and Rico, turning up his overcoat collar, leaned against it. It was after three o'clock and the streets were empty. Southward the lights of the Loop made a reddish glow in the sky.

At Sicily Pete's the mechanical piano was playing. Three men, all Italians, and two girls, both Americans, were sitting at a front table. They were drunk. They played with their food, spilled their coffee, and banged on the plates with their knives. Pete stood behind the counter, scowling.

When Rico came in he said:

"Hello, my friend, where have you been keeping yourself?"

"I haven't been around lately. Got some noisy birds, ain't you?"

Pete shrugged his shoulders.

"Yes, the fools. They drink gin. That is no drink for an Italian."

Rico took out his cigarettes and offered Pete one. They stood smoking. One of the girls pulled up her dress and fixed her garter. Rico smiled.

"Get an eyeful of that, Pete."

"Yes, yes," said Pete, "that's all I get, an eyeful. Every night I stand here while other people have a good time."

The girl looked up at Rico and he winked at her. She said to one of the men :

"Look at that smarty over there. He thinks he's cute."

The man looked foggily at Rico. Pete put his hand on Rico's arm.

"My friend, don't start no trouble, please. That's all we have around here, trouble. With one thing and another, I think I go back to Italy."

Rico turned his back on the girl.

"O.K.," he said.

While Pete was getting Rico a cup of coffee, a newsboy came in :

"EXTRA ! EXTRA ! All about the big hold-up."

Rico bought a paper and glanced at the three-inch headlines.

THUGS KILL CAPTAIN COURTNEY
IN CASA ALVARADO HOLD-UP

Rico showed Pete the paper.

"Another killing," he said.

"Yes," said Pete, "kill, kill, that's all they do. I wish to God I was back in Sicily. The Mafia, what is that? That is a kindergarten."

One of the Italians bought a paper and started to read the account of the hold-up aloud. All the people round the table stopped eating to listen. Rico sipped his coffee and watched them.

5

Tony hadn't slept all night. He lay in the cold dark room, sweating. The covers felt heavy as lead and from time to time he tossed them off, only to pull them over him again as the lake wind, streaming in the window, made him shiver. At intervals he would fall into a doze. Then he would see a windy street, feel a car skidding under him, feel a sickening jolt. He would wake with a start and sit up in bed.

"They'll get us for this," he kept repeating, "they'll get us sure."

Unable to control his imagination, he saw the high forbidding walls of the State Prison, the tiny death cells with their heavily-grated windows; then in the prison yard, the gallows. He remembered what Rico had said about Red Gus, on the night of his execution: "Well, they're gonna put a necktie on Gus he won't take off!" Yeah, they sure put a necktie on Gus.

Tony smoked cigarette after cigarette. In his despair he cast about for someone to put the blame on. It was all Midge's fault. Wasn't she always after him to make more jack so she could put on the dog? Hadn't he tried to go straight and drive a taxi and make an honest living? Yeah, and hadn't Sam Vettori and Rico offered him money to quit his job and give them a lift on their stick-ups? Well, you couldn't quit a gang; once you were in, you were in!

Tony sat up in bed and looked out across the roofs outside his window. The sun was coming up and a cold, windy winter morning was dawning. Of a sudden he began to feel sick at his stomach. He lay down, but that didn't help him, then he tossed from side to side.

He heard his mother moving about in the next room. She was getting dressed to go to work. An alarm-clock in a room across the court rang, then there was some loud swearing, and a window was slammed.

Tony had to vomit. He jumped out of bed and ran for the bathroom. When he came out his mother was lighting the stove.

She acted as if she didn't see him. He went back to his room but stopped in the doorway.

"Hello, mom," he said.

His mother paid no attention.

"Say," said Tony, "what's the matter?"

His mother turned and with her hands on her hips stared at him.

"Go back to bed, you loafer," she said, "I am sick of you. You are no good on earth. Just like your father."

"Aw, mom," said Tony.

"Don't try to salve me," said Tony's mother. "You go back to bed and get sober. You think I don't know nothing, don't you? Just like your father."

"I'm not drunk," said Tony, "I'm sick."

His mother turned her back and went on with her cooking. Tony went into his room, slammed the door, and got back into bed. A deadly depression settled on him. The world looked black.

He heard his mother go out, then he got up, dressed and made himself some toast and coffee. Anyway, he wanted his split.

On the way to Vettori's he met Father McConagha. The priest was a big man with a big, pale face. He walked with a rolling gait and there was something arrogant about him. Tony took off his hat.

"Good morning, Father."

"Good morning, Antonio," said Father McConagha. "Where have you been, my boy? I haven't seen you for months."

"I been working," said Tony.

"What sort of work?" asked Father McConagha, putting his hand on Tony's shoulder.

"I been driving a taxi."

The priest nodded his head slowly.

"That is good work, Antonio."

Tony couldn't look at Father McConagha and kept twisting his hat in his hands and staring at it. Father McConagha talked to him for a minute or two about the rewards of honesty and the happiness to be derived from doing your work faithfully, then he said:

"Antonio, one day your father asked me to look out for you. Your father was a good man, but weak. Remember this, Antonio, if you are ever in any trouble I am the one to come to."

Tony flushed and said:

"Thank you, Father."

When Father McConagha had gone, Tony began to speculate. Did he know anything? Why, on this very morning, had he said something about being in trouble? Tony respected and admired Father McConagha. He felt that he could always turn to him.

Talking with the priest had made him feel stronger, but now that the priest had gone all the hopelessness of the night before rushed back on him. He took out a cigarette and lit it with shaking hands.

"They'll get us sure for this," he said.

Then once more he began to think about Red Gus and what Rico had said about him.

6

SEAL SKIN couldn't get Otero sober. She made him eat tomatoes and she gave him a cold bath, but nothing seemed to do him any good. He walked about the flat in his underclothes singing songs in bastard Spanish and bragging about what a great, brave man he was. Only one man in the world braver: Rico.

Seal Skin was dead for sleep, but she didn't shut her eyes for fear Otero would do some crazy thing like shooting out the window at the street light (he had done this one night) or going out in his underclothes.

Otero sat at the table with his automatic beside him, singing at the top of his voice.

"Look," he cried, "I am Ramón Otero, a great, brave man. I ain't afraid of nobody or nothing. I can drink any man in the world under the table and I can outshoot any man that walks on two legs. Only Rico; he is my friend. He is a great man like Pancho Villa and I love him with a great love. I would not shoot Rico if he shot me first. Rico is my friend and I love him with a great love."

Then he got up and, snapping his fingers, began to dance, stamping with his heels, wiggling his hips, till Seal Skin nearly fell out of her chair laughing.

Toward morning he went to sleep with his head on the table. Seal Skin picked him up and carried him to bed (he weighed about a hundred and fifteen pounds), then, too tired to take off her clothes, she climbed in beside him.

7

Rico bought all the papers he could find and went up to his room to read them. He sat at his table, his hat tilted over his eyes, with a pair of scissors in his hand, cutting from the papers all the articles dealing with the hold-up and the killing of Police Captain Courtney. He arranged the clippings in a neat pile, then read them over and over.

One said:

. . . the thug who shot Police Captain Courtney was a small, pale foreigner, probably an Italian. He was dressed in a natty overcoat and a light felt hat.

Another:

. . . Courtney's murderer was described by one eyewitness as a small, unhealthy-looking foreigner.

Rico tore up this clipping.

"Where do they get that unhealthy stuff!" he said. "I never been sick a day in my life."

PART 3

I

SAM VETTORI's heavy, dark face looked puffy and his eyes were swollen. He hadn't been sleeping well lately and he had been drinking whiskey. As wine was his usual drink, the whiskey indicated a state of mind the reverse of calm. He sat chewing a cold stogie and from time to time pouring himself a shot from the bottle at his elbow. Rico was playing solitaire, his hat tilted over his eyes. The Big Boy sat opposite Vettori, his derby on the side of his head, and his huge fists, fists which at one time had swung a pick in a section gang, lying before him on the table.

The Big Boy shook his head from side to side slowly.

"Not a chance, Sam," he said, "I can't do nothing for you. Why, you must be out of your mind. Listen, they're after me hot and heavy. I got all I can do to take care of number one, see? Things was running too good for you, Sam. That's your trouble. You thought I was God himself. But listen, I ain't no miracle man. A stick-up more or less, what's that? But when it comes to plugging a bull like Courtney, that's out! No, Sam. You're on your own now. It ain't gonna be none too healthy for none of us for a while. Just don't lose your nerve, that's the main thing. Just hang on and watch the guys that are in the know."

"You leave that to me," said Rico without looking up.

"O.K.," said the Big Boy, "I think you're the goods, Rico. But don't get nervous with that gat of yours, or they'll put a necktie on you. Get this. No more stick-ups. No more jobs. Just lay low, all of you. If you run out of jack, I'll stake you. Now I got to beat it. Don't call me up no more, Sam. Because I can't do nothing for you and it might give the bulls an idea."

The Big Boy got to his feet and stood leaning his huge hairy paws on the table.

"Why, you guys are lucky and don't know it. Wood's manager got so goddamn rattled he identified one of the plain-clothes men as the guy that did the inside stand. Jesus, but it was rich! Spike Rieger was boiling. Pretty soon he pinned the manager down and the damn dummy said that the guys that did the job were Poles. So they went out and grabbed Steve Gollancz. Steve and his bunch had just tapped a bank and Steve thought they had the goods on him. It was funny as hell!"

The Big Boy put his head back and brayed. Sam Vettori drummed on the table irritably.

"All right, laugh," said Sam.

"Sure, I'll laugh," said the Big Boy; "if you'd seen Steve's face when he found out what it was all about you'd split your pants laughing."

"Steve's the goods," said Rico.

"You said a mouthful," said the Big Boy, "he's got them eating out of his hand. Well, I'm gonna beat it. You guys lay low and it might blow over. If things get hot, I'll tip off Scabby and then you all better hit the rods. So long."

The Big Boy went out slamming the door. They heard him go downstairs; he walked as heavily as a squad of police and banged each step with his heels.

Rico went on with his game of solitaire.

"Well," said Vettori, "something just tells me we're gonna get ours."

"Oh, hell!" said Rico, pushing the cards away from him, "I'd like to get the guy that invented that game."

Vettori swore softly to himself at Rico's indifference, then, pouring himself another drink, he said:

"You think Joe's safe, Rico."

"Yeah," said Rico, "as long as they don't nab him and put it to him. He can't stand the gaff."

"How about The Greek?"

Rico laughed.

"Safe as hell. Only thing with Otero, he gets lit and wants to raise hell. I had to knock him down a couple of times last night. He gets a little money and he goes nuts. That goddamn greaser never saw over five dollars all at once till I picked him up in Toledo. But he's safe."

"How about Tony?"

Rico didn't say anything for a minute but picked up his cards and began to shuffle them.

"I don't know about Tony."

Sam Vettori got up and walked back and forth, mopping his forehead at intervals with his big white silk handkerchief.

"Love of God, Rico, we can't take no chances with him."

Rico dealt out a couple of poker hands and began to play an imaginary game.

"You leave that to me, Sam," he said.

Vettori put his hand on Rico's shoulder.

"That's the talk, Rico. We get a break we may come clean."

Vettori dropped back into his chair and poured himself another drink, but Rico reached across the table and pushed the glass off on the floor.

"Slow down on that stuff, Sam. You got to keep your head clear."

Vettori looked at Rico in a fury, then he lowered his eyes.

"You got the right dope, Rico. That stuff don't do nobody no good."

Vettori took the whiskey bottle and locked it up in a cupboard.

2

About nine o'clock Carillo put his head in the door. Downstairs the jazzband had just started to play.

"Well?" demanded Vettori, getting to his feet.

"Blackie wants to see you," said Carillo.

"All right."

Carillo went out.

"What you suppose he wants?" said Vettori.

Rico, who was sitting with his chair tipped back against the wall reading a magazine, shook his head without looking up or answering. He was deep in the reading of a story about a rich society girl who fell in love with a bootlegger. Rico read everything he could find that had anything to do with society. He was fascinated by a stratum of existence which seemed so remote and unreal to him. The men of this level were "saps" and "softies" to him, but he envied them their women. He had seen them getting out of limousines at the doors of Gold Coast hotels. He had seen them, magnificently dressed, insolent, inaccessible, walking up the carpets under the canvas marquees. The door men would bow. The women would disappear. Rico hated them. They were so arrogant and self-sufficient, and they did not know that there was such a person in the world as Rico.

Blackie Avezzano, who managed Sam's garage, came in and shut the door behind him. He was small and bowlegged, and he was so dark that he had been taken for a mulatto many times.

Vettori impatiently exclaimed:

"Well, what's on your mind, Blackie?"

Rico went on reading his magazine. Blackie sat down at the table and seemed to be making an effort to collect his thoughts.

"All right, spit it out," said Vettori.

Blackie couldn't speak very good English, but as Rico didn't know a word of Italian and Vettori preferred to speak English, he did the best he could.

"Tony he took sick. Listen, I tell you, Tony he no know what. He took sick. I see him, listen, I tell you, what-you-say, he no got his guts. The Madre she send me call the doctor. Listen, he say, Tony, what-you-say, you been a drink. Now listen, you cut out a drink. That's all. Tony he no drink. What a hell! One bottle of beer he can no drink. He no got his guts, that's all."

Vettori looked at Rico, who went on reading.

"Rico," he said.

"I heard him," said Rico, "I ain't deaf."

Blackie got up and stood twisting his cap in his hand. Vettori took out his billfold and handed Blackie a ten.

"Blackie," he said, "keep your eyes open, understand?"

"All right," said Blackie, "I watch, see I know. Tony no good. All right I watch."

When he had gone Rico said:

"Well, that's that."

"We can't take no chances," said Vettori.

"I'll give him till tomorrow," said Rico; "he can't go far wrong with Blackie watching him. After that if he don't settle down, there won't be no more Tony."

3

Tony had always been of a rather easy-going nature and took things as they came. His emotions, it is true, were very unstable; with him anger was almost immediately followed by a grin, and depression lasted only long enough for him to recognize that he had felt such an emotion. No, he had never before experienced the loneliness which is the result of continued despair. Now he felt it and it was too much for him. He looked back on the past as a sort of fabulous period when he had had peace of mind.

He could enjoy nothing. The fear of arrest and hanging dogged him even at the movies, formerly his chief pleasure, and in the company of Midge, his woman, he was so preoccupied that she thought he had a new woman and treated him accordingly. Even the presence of his mother, who had begun to realize that something was wrong, did not tranquilize him. He drank, played pool, rode about in an automobile, but fear pursued him and he could find no rest.

Then he began to have attacks of acute indigestion, and it got so bad that the very sight of food was repugnant to him. He lost weight rapidly.

There was nothing he could do. He could not find one avenue of escape. But little by little the thought of Father McConagha took possession of him. Tony was too unintelligent to know that what he needed most of all was someone he could unburden himself to. But he blundered toward that solution.

Blackie's solicitude helped some. Blackie came to see him every night; and once, when Tony's indigestion had been worse than usual, he had even gone for the doctor.

Tony's mother put her hand on his shoulder.

"Antonio," she said, "I think I'll go over across the street and see Mrs. Mangia. She is having a new baby. Only think! That will be twelve."

Tony tried to smile.

"Twelve!" said Tony's mother, shaking her head slowly from side to side, "and one is too much."

"A bad egg like me is."

"You ain't a bad egg, Antonio," said his mother, "you are only lazy."

Tony said nothing.

"Listen, Antonio, I left some spaghetti on the stove. If you feel better eat some. You don't want to get all run down."

"All right," said Tony.

Tony's mother went out. As soon as the door was shut, Tony wished that she hadn't gone. He was afraid. At the sound of footsteps in the corridor, he felt his hair rise and beads of sweat stood out on his forehead. He got to his feet and began to walk up and down. A fury seized him; he cursed Rico and Vettori aloud. Then suddenly the anger left him and the fear returned.

Blackie put his head in the door.

"How you feel, Tony?" he asked.

"Hello, Blackie," said Tony, "come on in and have a smoke."

Blackie took a cigarette from the proffered pack and sat down. While he smoked he kept glancing at Tony.

"Whatsa mat, Tony?" said Blackie. "You ain't look so good."

Tony stared at Blackie for a moment, then he began to shake all over.

"Jesus, Blackie," he cried, "I can't stand it. They'll get us sure. Have you seen tonight's paper?"

Blackie shrugged.

"I can no read."

"It's all up with us," said Tony. "My God, I don't see how Rico stands it."

"Rico no scared."

"Well, he ought to be. He's the one that done it."

Blackie shrugged.

"No can help. What-you-say, Cortenni pull a gat. No can help."

Tony got very pale of a sudden. He heard an automobile stop in the street below. He ran to the window and looked down, then he turned and came back.

"I thought it was the cops," he said.

"Look," said Blackie, "you no better be sick. Listen, you no got your guts, Tony. Rico say, be a man. That is good. Be a man Rico say. You no better be sick."

"The hell with Rico," said Tony.

Blackie shrugged.

Tony stood in the middle of the room for a minute or two looking at the floor, then, suddenly making up his mind, he went over to the hatrack and got his hat.

"Where you go?" asked Blackie.

Tony hesitated.

"I go too," said Blackie.

"No, you go home," said Tony, then looking steadily at Blackie he said: "Me, I'm going down to St. Dominick's and see Father McConagha."

"What," cried Blackie, leaping up in alarm. "Tony, my God, you no tell him nothing."

"I got to," cried Tony vehemently.

Blackie took hold of Tony's arm.

"Tony, my boy, don't go. Listen, Tony, you no sick. Be a man. Hear what I tell you. You no live, see, you no live. Be a man."

Tony pushed him away.

"You go home, Blackie."

Tony went out. Blackie heard him walking slowly down the corridor. When he could no longer hear his footsteps, he leapt to his feet, opened a back window, went down the fire-escape, and took a short cut through the alleys. He knocked at the back door of the Palermo and Carillo let him in.

4

VETTORI stared at Rico, who said nothing.

"Crazy! Crazy!" said Blackie. "I tell him, be a man, be a man. But he say, I got to, I got to."

Rico hastily put on his overcoat.

"Well, I guess that's it," said Sam Vettori.

"Yeah," said Rico, "that's it. Now get yourself a can, Sam, and let's go. We ain't got any time to waste."

Vettori rubbed both hands over his face.

"Not me," he said.

Rico looked at him.

"Take Blackie," said Vettori.

Blackie implored them with his eyes.

"Blackie's no good," said Rico.

"No," said Blackie, "I no good."

Carillo put his head in the door.

"Reilley's downstairs, boss."

"Take Carillo," said Vettori.

Carillo stared at them suspiciously. Rico leapt across the room and grabbed him by the arm.

"Listen, Bat, can you drive a can?"

"Sure."

"Will you let her out when I office you?"

"Sure."

"All right, let's go."

"Take that black roadster, Carillo," said Vettori, "but for God's sake don't smash it up."

Carillo ran out leaving the door open. Rico walked over and closed the door, then he said :

"Sam, you ain't got any more guts than Tony. Now listen, get down there and talk turkey to Reilley. Get that! By God, I guess I got to boss this job myself."

Vettori looked at Rico with hatred. But he said :

"All right, Rico, you're the boss now."

Rico went out. Blackie said :

"Goodbye Tony!"

Carillo was waiting with the black roadster in the alley-way. Rico jumped in and the roadster leapt away. Carillo took a turn on two wheels.

"It's a cinch he went the shortest cut," said Rico.

"Sure," said Carillo, "I know what I'm doing."

"All right," said Rico, "do it."

The wind had risen and it began to snow, big, heavy flakes

which sailed past the street lights. In a few minutes the ground was covered.

Carillo took the shortest cut and Rico, holding his big automatic on the seat beside him, sat straining his eyes. But there was no sign of Tony.

"If we miss him I'll kick hell out of Blackie," said Rico.

"Keep your shirt on, boss," said Carillo.

The tall spires of St. Dominick's rose before them at the end of the block. The street was deserted. Carillo drove slowly now, hugging the kerb. In a moment he pointed:

"There's a guy."

Rico leaned forward.

"Take it easy, Bat," he said, "I think it's Tony."

Carillo throttled down to five miles an hour. The man, a dim black figure in the falling snow, stopped in front of the cathedral and looked up. When the automobile came abreast of him he turned.

"Tony," called Rico.

"Yeah?" came Tony's voice, "Who is it?"

Rico fired. A long spur of flame shot out in the darkness. Rico emptied his gun. Tony fell without a sound.

"All right now, Bat," said Rico, "let her out."

5

JOE and Olga were sitting in a quiet corner of a Gold Coast hotel dining-room. They were waiting for their dessert. Joe, comfortably full and inclined to be amiable, sat looking at Olga. She was the goods. Of course he stepped out with other broads occasionally when Olga was busy, but that didn't count. Olga was the goods and she was his woman. Other men didn't rate with her, that's all. He studied her. There she sat with her round dark face, her high cheekbones, and her dark mascara-ed eyes. Her long thin fingers covered with rings fascinated him. Her slimness, her elegance made him feel very uncouth and protective and masculine.

"Well," said Olga, "take a good look."

"Listen, baby," said Joe, "you got it. I ain't kidding. You

got everything. There ain't a woman in Chicago that's got half your stuff. You make 'em all look silly."

Olga reached across the table and patted his hand.

"I don't believe it, but say it again. I like it."

"No fooling."

"What a line," said Olga.

The waiter brought their dessert.

"I'll tell you," said Olga, looking at her wrist watch, "let's go to a movie. I got time."

Joe didn't like movies very well; all that sappy love stuff! But now he wanted to please Olga.

"All right. Where'll it be?"

Olga turned to the waiter.

"Bring us a paper, please."

The waiter brought a paper and handed it to Joe. He unfolded it and started to turn to the theatrical page, but instead he read with absorption an article on the front page. Olga saw him swallow several times. When he glanced up at her there was a bewildered look in his eyes and his face had begun to get pale.

"What's wrong?" she asked.

"They got Tony," said Joe.

"Who?"

"I don't know. Rico, I guess. He must have turned yellow."

Joe ran his hand across his forehead, then he took out his gold cigarette case, but without ostentation this time, and lit a cigarette. Olga took the paper from him. She read:

ANOTHER GANG KILLING

Antonio Passalacqua, known as Tony Passa, reputed to be a member of the Vettori gang, was found dead near the steps of St. Dominick's Cathedral . . . as far as the police can ascertain no one saw him killed . . . when questioned Sam Vettori denied all knowledge of the shooting and intimated that it was the work of a rival gang . . . police say that this is likely.

"Jesus!" said Joe.

Olga turned quickly to the theatrical page.

"Joe, honey," she said, "there's a good comedy at the Oriental. What do you say?"

Joe crumpled up his cigarette and put it in the ash-tray.

"Boy, Rico didn't waste no time with him."
"Joe, don't you want to see that comedy?"
"Sure," said Joe, "let's go see it."
Joe sat silent in the taxi all the way to the theatre. As they were getting out, he said :
"Boy, that Rico is sure careless with a rod."
"Forget it, honey," said Olga.

6

WHEN Rico came in Seal Skin was sitting in a chair by the window and Otero was lying on the bed without his shirt, singing loudly. Rico walked over and put his hand on Seal Skin's shoulder.

"Listen," he said, "I thought you told me you was gonna look after The Greek?"

"I can't do nothing with him," said Seal Skin.

"Señor Rico," cried Otero, "listen, I will sing for you."

Rico turned.

"Seal," he said, "that bird's gonna spill something if you don't keep him sober."

"Listen," said Seal Skin, "I ain't no nurse. A guy ought to look out for himself. What the hell can I do, anyway? I can't knock him cold."

"You never did have much sense," said Rico.

"All right, wise boy. Let's see what you can do."

Rico took off his overcoat.

"Got any ice?"

"Sure," said Seal Skin without moving.

"Well, goddamn it, get on your feet and get it."

Seal Skin was afraid of Rico but she didn't want him to suspect it. She got to her feet leisurely, picked up one of Otero's big cigars, lit it, and stood puffing. Then, having demonstrated her lack of fear, she went to the kitchen for the ice.

Rico went over to the bed.

"Otero," he said, "have you got any liquor around here?"

"What do I care for liquor!" cried Otero. "I will sing for you."

Rico slapped Otero's face.

"A hell of a crew I'm mixed up with," he said.

Otero looked at him, startled.

"What is wrong with me?"

"You're a dirty yellow bum."

"I am not a yellow bum," cried Otero, trying to sit up.

Rico struck him hard this time, knocking him back on the bed. Otero put his hand to his face and looked at Rico.

"If you got any more liquor here you better tell me where it is," said Rico.

Otero reached under his pillow, and pulled out a quart bottle over half full. Rico slipped it into his pocket.

Otero's face got red.

"Rico," he said, "you give me back my liquor."

He tried to sit up but Rico hit him and he fell back. Seal Skin came in with a couple of pieces of ice wrapped in a towel.

"What the hell you want to beat him up for?" she said.

"I'm gonna get him sober and keep him that way."

"Yeah? Well, you're gonna have a full time job."

Rico took the ice, a piece in each hand, and began to rub it over Otero's face and chest. He rubbed hard and it hurt Otero, who struggled.

"Rico," he said, "what have I done to you? Rico, you are my friend. Why do you treat me this way?"

"He'll be bawling next," said Seal Skin.

Of a sudden Otero got angry and struggled so fiercely that he threw Rico off and climbed out of bed. The ice clattered to the floor. Rico took one step toward him and set himself for a punch, but Seal Skin grabbed his arm.

"For God's sake let up on him," she cried, "ain't he in bad enough shape?"

Rico was furious. He slapped Seal Skin across the face with his open hand.

"A fine bunch of yellow bellies and squealers I'm mixed up with," he cried. "Listen, idiot, ain't he a meal ticket? You want the black wagon to come and haul him away?"

Otero reeled across the room. Rico leapt after him and knocked him to the floor. Otero raised his head.

"Rico," he said, "what have I done to you?"

Rico picked up the ice and kneeling down beside Otero began to rub him with it, harder than before. Otero gasped.

"Listen," said Rico, "you got to get sober. I'm your friend, Otero, do you get what I'm saying? You got to sober up and stay that way."

Tears ran down Otero's cheeks.

"All right, Rico," he said.

In half an hour Rico had him sober. Seal Skin was sitting with her feet on the window sill, smoking one of Otero's big cigars. Otero sat pale and shaken, looking at Rico.

"Well, big boy," said Seal Skin, "I got to hand it to you. You done it."

Rico smiled. Then he took out his billfold and handed Seal Skin a ten.

"There's a little cush for you. You ain't sore at me cause I socked you, are you? I got red hot mad, that's all."

"You didn't sock me hard," said Seal Skin, "but it was ten dollars' worth."

Otero didn't have much to say. He sat looking at the floor, ashamed of himself.

"How do you feel?" asked Rico.

"Me, not so good," said Otero.

"Want a little drink."

Otero looked at Rico, not trusting him, then he nodded. Rico handed him the bottle.

"I said little drink," cautioned Rico.

Otero took a swallow and handed back the bottle.

"Now," said Rico, "get your clothes on and we'll take a look at Tony."

7

THERE were many rumours in Little Italy about the passing of Sam Vettori. The full truth, of course, was only guessed at, but the simple facts were known. Sam Vettori's star was setting, Rico's was rising. Rico had always been right; there was never any question of that. Rico had always inspired fear. But now, as the probable head of a big minor gang whose activities were varied and whose yearly income was enormous, his potentialities were prodigiously increased and he was treated accordingly.

When he entered Tony's flat several members of the Vettori gang, sitting near the door, got up and offered him their chairs. He merely shook his head and walked across to where Sam Vettori was sitting. Otero, who had entered a little behind Rico, stopped to talk with Blackie Avezzano.

Carillo brought a chair for Rico and Rico sat down beside Sam Vettori.

"We're going to plant the kid right," said Vettori, "that'll look good."

Rico stared across the room at a large horseshoe wreath which bore the single word: Tony. That was his contribution.

"Sure," said Rico.

He was a little uneasy. Not that he felt any remorse. What he had done was merely an act of policy. A man in this game must be a man. If he gets yellow, why, there's only one remedy for it. No, Rico was never likely to err on the side of contrition. It was the massed flowers; their sickly and overpowering odour made him vaguely uneasy.

"They sure fix 'em up good now," said Vettori, nodding in the direction of the coffin; "he don't look dead. He looks like he was asleep."

"Yeah?" said Rico.

"It beats me how they do it," said Vettori.

Carillo came across the room and whispered to Rico and Vettori.

"Two bulls in the hallway."

"They coming in?" asked Rico.

"No, just standing there."

"All right."

There was a movement at the door. Mrs. Passalacqua came in between two of her friends. She had been at St. Dominick's for over an hour. Rico got up and offered her his chair. One of the women helped her off with her hat. She sat down. Her grey hair was parted in the middle and drawn tightly down;

her face was a dead white. She was wearing a plain black dress and she sat with her hands in her lap. She looked at no one, but fastened her eyes on the coffin.

Rico walked over to look at Tony. At the head of the coffin were two big candles, one of them leaning a little and dripping tallow. Tony lay with his hands folded. Rico looked down. Somehow he had expected Tony to be changed. He was not. Here lay the same Tony who used to play poker with such fury. The same Tony, yes, only dead. Rico saw the rigidity of the face, the parchment skin. He stood there, looking.

Carillo put his hand on Rico's shoulder.

"Bulls want to see you, boss."

Rico nodded.

"They want you to come out in the hall."

"All right," said Rico, turning away from the coffin, "tell Otero."

Otero came over beside Rico and stood looking at Tony.

"Listen," said Rico, "this may be a pinch. I don't know. If it is, I'll go with them. They ain't got nothing on me. But if there's any trouble, Scabby'll keep you posted. Ma's got my jack, see?"

"All right," said Otero.

Rico started across the room and Otero followed him. Before Rico reached the door Tony's mother suddenly put her hands to her face and began to sob wildly.

"Oh, Tony, Tony!" she cried.

The women who had come in with her tried to quiet her, but she pushed them away, and, rising, walked over to the coffin and stood looking down at Tony. Then, still sobbing, she let the women lead her into the next room.

"That's a woman for you," said Rico.

"Well," said Otero, shrugging, "Tony was her son."

The hallway was lined with poor Italians who, not knowing the Passalacquas, had come out of curiosity. They stood in silent groups, trying to peep in through the open door. Women in disreputable housedresses carrying dirty children; pregnant women; old men with crinkly grey hair and seamed brown faces; young girls trying to look up-to-date and American. When Rico came out they all stared at him.

Flaherty took hold of his arm.

"Rico," he said, "come down to the end of the hall. I want to see you a minute."

"Is this a pinch?" asked Rico.

Flaherty laughed.

"Got a bad conscience, have you? Well, you ought to have."

Rico noticed that the other detective, whom he had never seen before, kept staring at him. Rico planted his feet firmly and stared back.

"What's the big idea, Flaherty?" he asked.

"Well," said Flaherty, "just to put your mind at rest I'll tell you, this ain't a pinch. It ought to be, but it ain't. Now will you take a walk . . .?"

"Sure," said Rico.

Otero came out into the hallway and stood watching them. Rico went down to the end of the hall with the two plain-clothes men. Some of the poor Italians followed them and stood staring. But Flaherty motioned them off as if he were shooing chickens.

"Beat it," he said; "go tend to your own business."

They moved away slowly, looking back.

"All right," said Rico, "let's have it."

Flaherty took out a big cigar and began chewing on it. The other man kept staring. Rico was puzzled and wondered what the game was; then he noticed that the light at their end of the hall was good, much better than any other place in the hall. The once-over? Well, what then.

"Listen, Rico," said Flaherty, "I like you and I'm going to give you a tip. It's going to be tough on you birds from now on. The Old Man's got his back up. Now get this. If you got anything on your mind, you better spill it." Flaherty paused to light his cigar. The other detective watched Rico intently. "Because it's going to be easy for the bird that spilled it first. But God help the rest of them."

"Quit stalling," he said.

Flaherty glanced at the man with him, but the man shook his head. Flaherty said:

"Well, I'm giving you a friendly tip."

"Yeah," said Rico, "you bulls always was friendly as hell. I spent two years once just thinking how friendly you was. Listen, I ain't got nothing to spill. What the hell's wrong with you, Flaherty? Did I ever do any spilling?"

Flaherty laughed.

"Well," he said, "there's a first time for everything. All right, Rico, you can go."

The two plain-clothes men pushed their way through the crowd and went down the stairs. Rico went back into Tony's flat. Sam Vettori and Otero were waiting for him. Vettori was mopping his face with his big white silk handkerchief.

"Well?" he demanded.

Rico shrugged.

"Just stalling."

"What's the name?"

"You got me. I guess Flaherty wanted this other bird to give me the once-over."

"Things getting pretty hot, Rico."

"Don't beef, Sam. We're gonna come through."

Otero said:

"The old lady sure is taking it hard."

They could hear Tony's mother sobbing loudly in the next room.

PART 4

I

For three or four years Bat Carillo, once a third-rate light-heavyweight, had been the leader of one of Vettori's gangs of hooligans. The members of this gang specialized in strong arm stuff and intimidation; they threw bombs; they smashed up bar-rooms and vice-joints operated by rival gangs. They were, in other words, Vettori's shock troops. Carillo was an excellent lieutenant, as he always carried out orders to the letter; and was congenitally incapable of imagining himself as chief in his own right. A good honest subordinate without ambition. Vettori trusted him.

In Carillo's attitude since the killing of Courtney, therefore, Vettori saw the most unmistakable symptom of his own passing. Carillo had attached himself to Rico and called him "boss." Carillo was not careless with the word "boss"; it was not a conventional expression; when he said "boss" he meant it. Aroused, Vettori saw similar manifestations all around him; in Blackie Avezzano, in Killer Pepi, in a dozen others.

Vettori had always disliked Rico. Now he hated him. If Carillo or Killer Pepi had remained faithful he would have had one of them kill him and damn the consequences. But there was no question of that now. He knew that he was whipped and he saw the necessity of a compromise. Hanging was just over the horizon and Rico's gun promised an even more certain death. Vettori had never split with anyone. He had always taken with both hands and given as little as possible. But it was split now or die and Vettori could not contemplate the prospect of dying with any degree of complacency. He sent for Rico.

A new Rico appeared, followed by Otero, Carillo, and Killer Pepi. Rico was wearing a big ulster like Joe's and a derby also like Joe's. He had on fawn-coloured spats drawn over pointed patent-leather shoes; and a diamond horseshoe pin sparkled in a red, green and white striped necktie.

Vettori looked him over and winked at Killer Pepi, but Killer Pepi's face was stony. Carillo got a chair for Rico.

"What's on your mind, Sam?" said Rico, sitting down, throwing back his ulster and pulling up his trousers to preserve the crease.

Vettori hesitated.

"I want to see you alone," he said.

"No," said Rico, "I think I know your game, Sam, and I want the boys to get an earful. Go ahead and spill it."

Vettori began to sweat. Killer Pepi said:

"Yeah, we know."

"You know a hell of a lot, don't you?" said Vettori.

"We know, all right," said Pepi.

Nobody said anything. Rico took off his hat and began to comb his hair. Vettori got out his cards and began to lay out a game of solitaire.

Pepi said:

"We know you went yellow, Sam, when Tony blew his top and started after Come-To-Jesus McConagha. We know all right."

Vettori looked up at him.

"What the hell I got you guys for anyway! Who hands out the cush?"

Rico paused in the combing of his hair.

"Don't get rough, Sam."

Killer Pepi went over and stood with his back against the door. Otero sat down opposite Vettori.

"Well," said Rico, "if you want to see me, spill it quick because I ain't got all night."

Vettori sighed profoundly, then he put down his cards and looked at the men around him. He saw four hostile faces.

"All right," said Vettori, "but why the strong arm stuff, Rico? Sit down, you guys, and I'll have some drinks sent up."

The three men looked at Rico.

"All right," he said, "go bring up some drinks, Bat."

Carillo went out. Nobody said anything. Outside, a winter dusk settled and the big electric sign on a level with the windows was switched on. They sat looking at the sign.

CLUB
P
A
L
E
R
M
O
DANCING

Carillo brought in the drinks and they all sat around the table under the green-shaded lamp. Otero, Carillo, and Killer Pepi drank whiskey; Vettori wine; Rico pop.

Vettori put down his glass.

"Well, Rico," he said, "I got a proposition to make you."

"All right," said Rico, "spring it."

"Listen," said Vettori, "I'm getting old. I'll never see forty-five again, and when a guy's that old he ain't worth much."

"You ain't getting old, Sam, you're losing your guts," said Rico.

Killer Pepi laughed out aloud and banged his fist on the table. But Vettori swallowed this insult.

"All right, Rico," he said, "that's your story. Well, here's how it is. I need a partner. You're young, Rico, and you got the guts. All the guys like you and they'll do what you say. I got the lay-out and you're looking for a chance to be a big guy. Well, here's your chance." Vettori thought for a moment, then he said : "I'll split the works with you."

Carillo and Pepi exchanged a look. Otero began to hum to himself. But Rico said :

"I'll think it over."

Vettori began to sweat again. Was Rico going to get rid of him?

"Well," he said, putting on a front, "you can take it or leave it. I like you, Rico, and I'm doing you a favour. Who's got the money? Who's got the pull? What the hell would you guys do if you didn't have the Big Boy to pull you through?"

"I'm O.K. with the Big Boy," said Rico, "he was up to see me this morning."

"Yeah," said Pepi, "I brung him."

Vettori laid out a new game of solitaire.

"Here's the thing," said Rico: "you're trying to hang on, Sam. You must think we're dumb as hell. You want me to do the work so you can take it easy. And you call that an even split. Hear what I say! That ain't my idea of a split."

"Well, I ain't handing out charity," said Vettori, losing his temper.

Rico got to his feet and buttoned up his ulster.

"All right, Sam."

Vettori slammed down his cards.

"What do you guys think?" he demanded of Carillo, Pepi and Otero.

"Ain't that a fair split?"

They just looked at him.

"No," said Rico, "I guess we can't do no business."

Rico put on his hat and walked toward the door. The other three got up and followed him. Vettori stood up.

"Well," he said, "you gonna try to run me out, Rico?"

Vettori was panicky. Rico stood at the door and looked at him.

"I was just figuring I'd open a joint across the street," he said.

Vettori knew what he meant. He had been through half a dozen gang wars, but that was long ago when there were at least five separate gangs in the neighbourhood. Things had been comparatively quiet for over three years. Vettori regretted the past bitterly. He regretted having taken up with Rico, an unknown Youngstown wop.

"Well," he said, "Rico, you're young and you ain't got any too much sense. What the hell! With things the way they are, we wouldn't none of us last a month. Listen, Rico, what's your idea of a split?"

Rico took off his hat and scratched his head, but carefully so that his hair wouldn't be disarranged.

"I'll hand you this, Sam," said Rico, "you got the lay-out.

The split's good that way. But you got sense enough to know that no two guys can run things. The lay-out split is O.K. with me, but I got to have the say, get that!"

Vettori looked at the others.

"What do you guys say?"

"We're in with Rico," said Killer Pepi.

Otero and Carillo nodded. Vettori brought his hand down on the table with a smack.

"O.K.," he said.

2

THE gang gave a banquet for Rico in one of Sam Vettori's big back rooms. The table was fifteen feet long and was covered by a fine white cloth. Red, green and white streamers hung from the chandeliers and Italian and American flags were crossed at intervals along the walls. At eleven o'clock the notables began to arrive. Killer Pepi in a blue suit and a brown derby, with his woman, Blue Jay, on his arm. Joe Sansone, gunman, and ex-lightweight, in a tuxedo, followed by his shadow, Kid Bean, a Sicilian, dark as a negro. Then Ottavio Vettori, Sam's cousin, not yet twenty-one, already famous as a gunman and spoken of as a potential gang chief. Then Otero, Blackie Avezzano and Bat Carillo, all with their women. They stood about stiffly, a little uncomfortable in their fine clothes, and tried to make conversation. The men, like all specialists, talked shop. Ottavio Vettori declared that the police were a bunch of bums. Killer Pepi agreed that they were. Joe Sansone said that the Federal men were just as bad, only smarter and crookeder. Killer Pepi agreed that they were. Ottavio Vettori didn't agree. He said that the Federal men were dumber and harder to fix. This brought on an argument.

When Sam Vettori came in the men were all shouting.

"What the hell!" said Sam, "ain't this a fine way to act at a banquet? You act like a bunch of gashouse micks. Cut the chatter."

Ottavio made a noise like a goat.

"Baa! Baa!"

Everybody laughed. Otero took out a quart bottle of

whiskey, drank from it and passed it to Seal Skin; she drank and passed it to Ottavio. The bottle circled the room and returned empty.

"You sure came prepared, you birds," said Sam. "Did any of you guys bring a lunch?"

"Baa! Baa!" bellowed Ottavio.

"My God, ain't that cute!" said Killer Pepi's girl.

"Hell, that ain't nothing," said Pepi, "listen." Pepi put three fingers in his mouth and blew a blast that made their eardrums ring.

"Lord," said Ottavio, "the cops! Baa! Baa!"

Three waiters came in, each carrying two quarts of whiskey. They put the bottles on the table and went out.

"That's an appetizer," said Sam.

"Apéritif," Joe Sansone corrected.

Ottavio slapped him on the back.

"What's that, little Joe? What the hell lingo is that?"

Joe pushed him away.

"You dumb birds don't you know nothing. Swell people don't say appetizer; they say apéritif."

"The hell they do! Well, I expect you know all about it. You used to be a bellboy at the Blackstone."

Everybody laughed. Killer Pepi blew a blast on his fingers. His girl looked at him admiringly.

"How the hell you ever learn to do that?"

"Aw, that ain't nothing."

"Say, Sam," said Carillo, "when do we eat?"

"When the boss gets here," said Pepi.

"Well, he better step on it because I'm so hungry I could eat dynamite," said Ottavio.

"Keep your shirt on," said Pepi.

"Haven't got an old soup sandwich in your pocket, have you?" asked Ottavio.

Everybody laughed. Ottavio was the recognized wit of the Vettori gang. All that he had to do to get a laugh was to open his mouth.

Sam Vettori took one of the quarts from the table and sent it round the room. It came back empty.

"What the hell you suppose is keeping Rico?" asked Carillo.

"Keep your shirt on," said Pepi.

"I go see," said Otero.

As he went out, the Big Boy came in. He had on a big racoon coat and his derby was on the side of his head. Sam Vettori rushed over and shook hands with him.

"What the hell you doing here?" he demanded.

"Me, I came to see the fun. Thinks are looking up, Sam. Things sure to God are looking up. I think we got 'em whipped."

Sam Vettori smiled broadly and poured the Big Boy a drink. Well, well! If the Courtney business blew over he was sitting pretty. All things considered, he hadn't done so bad. Time after time he had seen old gang leaders go down before younger men. But here he was hanging on, getting a 50-50 split, and taking no chances. Rico was the goods. Goddamn him and all his kind, but he was the goods.

"Yeah," said the Big Boy, "you got the Old Man on the run and Flaherty's about ready to do the Dutch Act. It's gonna blow over, Sam. You heard me speak. It's gonna blow over. I want to see Rico."

"He ain't showed yet," said Sam.

"Damn smart boy," said the Big Boy.

Sam smiled.

"Yeah," he said, pouring the Big Boy another drink, "damn smart kid. He's young yet, but I can show him the ropes."

The Big Boy didn't say anything. He just looked at Vettori.

Otero came running in, followed by two waiters, one of whom was carrying a big ulster and a derby; the other was carrying a woman's fur coat.

"Here he comes," cried Otero.

Kid Bean, who had collected a crowd in the middle of the room, and was walking on his hands to amuse them (he had once been an acrobat), jumped hastily to his feet and backed up against the wall. The crowd followed him. Killer Pepi said :

"All right now. Everybody yell like hell when he comes in."

Rico came in slowly, talking to Blondy Belle, the swellest woman in Little Italy. She was a handsome Italian, bold and aquiline. Her complexion and eyes were dark, but her hair, naturally black, was blondined, and this gave her an incongruous and a somewhat formidable appearance.

Rico was greeted by an uproar, pierced by Killer Pepi's shrill whistle. The Big Boy went to meet Rico and shook hands with him. Sam Vettori smiled and nodded, very affable, then went out to get things started. The Big Boy said to Blondy Belle :

"Got yourself a regular man, did you?"

Blondy took hold of Rico's arm.

"Surest thing you know."

The Big Boy laughed.

"What'd you do with Little Arnie?"

Rico took out a cigar and bit off the end.

"She ditched him," he said.

The Big Boy meditated. Blondy Belle had been Little Arnie's woman for a long time. Little Arnie ran the biggest gambling joint on the North Side, but he had been slipping for a year or more. He wasn't right; nobody could trust him.

"How did Little Arnie take it?" asked the Big Boy.

"He took it standing up," said Blondy Belle.

"Well, what could he do?" said Rico.

Killer Pepi, Ottavio Vettori and Joe Sansone, as the most important men in the gang next to Sam Vettori, came over to shake hands with Rico.

"A million dollars ain't in it with you," said Pepi, looking his boss over.

Rico was wearing a loud striped suit and a purple tie. He still had on his gloves, yellow kid, of which he was very proud, and his diamond horseshoe pin had been replaced by a big ruby surrounded by little diamonds. Ottavio envied him his gloves. But Joe Sansone was not impressed; he knew better.

"Yes sir, boss, you sure are lit up," said Ottavio.

"Here's the half-pint," said Killer Pepi, pushing Joe Sansone forward.

Joe shook hands with Rico.

"Yes sir," said Ottavio, "the half-pint's a good boy, but he and Gentleman Joe're too swell for us."

Rico looked around the room.

"Joe Massara here?"

"Ain't seen him," said Pepi.

"He won't be here," said Joe Sansone; "he's busy."

Rico didn't say anything. Blondy took hold of his arm.

"I want a drink."

Rico looked at Pepi.

"Get her a drink," he said.

The Big Boy took Rico aside and said :

"I want to see you a minute, Rico."

Rico said :

"Listen, if you see Joe Massara tomorrow you tell him to look me up. I got something to say to that bird."

"I'll be seeing him maybe," said the Big Boy. "I got a date with his boss tomorrow morning. There's a square guy, Rico. DeVoss is a square guy all right. Never have to nudge him for dough."

Rico seemed in a bad humour.

"They tell me you lined up something good," said the Big Boy.

Rico nodded.

"Yeah, it's gonna be a money maker. Little Arnie wised me up. I'm gonna give him a split. That's the game now. Sam never had sense enough to get in on it."

"Little Arnie, eh? That guy'd double-cross his grandmother."

"He'll only double-cross me once," said Rico.

"I believe you," said the Big Boy; then, putting his hand on Rico's shoulder, he went on : "Funny for you to split with Arnie. How about Blondy?"

"Arnie don't give a damn. He's all shot to pieces. He can't do a woman no good."

"No wonder," said the Big Boy, "with a woman like that."

Rico grinned.

"Ain't she a bearcat !" he said; then his face clouded. "Wonder what the hell Joe Massara's game is?"

The Big Boy looked at Rico for a moment.

"That little hunky dancer over at DeVoss's has got him down. They tell me he's going straight."

Rico laughed unpleasantly.

"Yeah? Well, I'll have to go over and give that bird an earful."

"Better stay out of that end of town, Rico."

"To hell with that."

Sam Vettori came in, followed by three waiters bringing the soup.

"All right," said Sam, "we're all set."

Rico took his place at the head of the table. The Big Boy sat on his right and Blondy Belle on his left. The gunmen and their women arranged themselves according to rank. Blackie Avezzano sat at the foot of the table.

3

WHEN the meal was over the Big Boy asked Rico to make a speech. There was a prolonged clamour. Rico got up.

"All right," he said, "if you birds want me to make a speech, here you are : I want to thank you guys for this banquet. It sure is swell. The liquor is good, so they tell me, I don't drink it myself, and the food don't leave nothing to be desired. I guess we all had a swell time and it sure is good to see all you guys gathered together. Well, I guess that's about all. Only I wish you guys wouldn't get drunk and raise hell, as that's the way a lot of birds get bumped off."

Rico sat down. The applause lasted for over a minute. Then Ottavio got up with a bottle in his hand.

"Here's to Rico and Blondy and the Big Boy."

Everybody shouted and made a grab for bottles and glasses. Blackie Avezzano fell under the table and stayed there, lying on his face. After the toast was drunk, Killer Pepi and Kid Bean began to quarrel. The Kid picked up a plate and struck at Pepi, who threw a bottle at the Kid, missing him by a fraction of an inch.

Rico banged on the table.

"Cut it out, you guys. Ain't that a hell of a way to act?"

Pepi and the Kid shook hands and another toast was drunk.

A waiter came in the door and went over to Rico.

"Couple of newspaper guys, boss. They want to take a flashlight."

"What's the idea?" the Big Boy inquired.

"Send 'em up," said Rico.

"We're gonna get our mugs shot," cried Blondy Belle.

"Maybe we are," said Rico.

"What's the idea?" the Big Boy reiterated.

"We ain't got nothing to hide," said Rico.

The waiter returned, followed by two newspaper men, one of whom was carrying a big camera. Rico motioned them over.

"Who sent you?" he asked.

Sam Vettori came in and went over to Rico.

"They're O.K., Rico," he said, "they been here before."

"Sure, we're O.K.," said the photographer, a little intimidated by Rico's manner.

"Well, spill it," said Rico, "what's the idea of the flashlight?"

"Well, we got a section in the Sunday paper about how different classes of people live in Chicago. See? Last week we featured Lake Forest. Had some pictures of the swells, see, and the dumps where they lived. This Sunday we want Little Italy. We just heard about the banquet they were giving you, Mr. Rico, so we kinda thought..."

"O.K.," said Rico, "but make it snappy."

"I'm out of this picture," said the Big Boy, rising and walking over to the doorway. Sam Vettori took his place.

After manoeuvring about for a few minutes the photographer got the correct slant. He put the powder on the little tray.

"Now!" he cried.

Rico sat with his thumbs in the arm-holes of his vest, looking very stern. There was a blinding flash. Ottavio Vettori leapt into the air and crying "My God, I'm shot" fell face down across the table. Everybody laughed.

When the newspaper men had gone the Big Boy came over and put his hand on Rico's arm.

"They may pick you up on that."

"Who the hell's gonna see it."

"You don't know who's gonna see it. That was a bad play, Rico."

Rico laughed.

"If they pick me up, I'll alibi them to death."

When the banquet was over Rico had Otero call him a cab. Blondy Belle was a little drunk and Rico had to support her as they went down the stairs. As she weighed about twenty pounds more than he did, this was not an easy job. As they were going out the side-entrance, Flaherty left his table in the club and came over to them.

He put his hand on Rico's shoulder.

"Getting up in the world ain't you, Rico?"

Rico looked at him.

"Don't you know your pal Jim Flaherty?"

"Sure I know you. What's the big idea?"

"Go chase yourself around the block, flat-foot," said Blondy Belle; "if I ain't getting sick of seeing bulls."

"Hello, Blondy," said Flaherty, "you and Rico hitting it off, eh? That's the old ticket. Rico's a good boy, but he's young. If they don't put him behind the bars, he'll be a man yet."

"What's the idea, Flaherty?" asked Rico.

"Why, I don't want you to forget that I'm your friend," said Flaherty. "I got my eyes on you, Rico. I like to see a young guy getting up in the world."

"Yeah?" said Rico.

The cab was waiting at the kerb and one of the waiters went out and opened the door for them. Rico boosted Blondy Belle into the cab. Flaherty stood in the doorway and watched them drive off.

"The nerve of that Irish bastard," said Blondy.

But Rico had forgotten Flaherty. He sat thinking about Joe Massara. Gentleman Joe was getting too good for them, eh? He was going to turn softie.

"Well, I guess not," said Rico.

4

THE sound of the pianola woke Rico. He sat up and looked at his wrist watch. It was two o'clock in the afternoon. He had slept twelve hours.

Rico lived at a tension. His nervous system was geared up

to such a pitch that he was never sleepy, never felt the desire, to relax, was always keenly alive. He did not average over five hours sleep a night and as soon as he opened his eyes he was awake. When he sat in a chair he never thrust out his feet and lolled, but sat rigid and alert. He walked, ate, took his pleasures in the same manner. What distinguished him from his associates was his ability to live in the present. He was like a man on a long train journey to a promised land. To him the present was but a dingy way-station; he had his eyes on the end of the journey. This is the mental attitude of a man destined for success. But the resultant tension had its drawbacks. He was subject to periodic slumps. His energy would suddenly disappear; he would lose interest in everything and for several days would sleep twelve to fifteen hours at a stretch. This was a dangerous weakness, and Rico was aware of it and feared it.

Rico leapt out of bed and hastily put on his clothes.

"Twelve hours, boy," he said to his reflection in the mirror, as he stood combing his hair, "that'll never do."

He had been seeing too much of Blondy Belle; that was the trouble. Rico had very little to do with women. He regarded them with a sort of contempt; they seemed so silly, reckless and purposeless, also mendacious and extremely undependable. Not that Rico trusted men, far from it. He was temperamentally suspicious. But in the course of his life he had discovered a few men he could trust, but no women. What he feared most in women, though, was not their treachery, that could be guarded against, but their ability to relax a man, to make him soft and slack, like Joe Massara. Rico had never been deeply involved with a woman. Incapable of tender sentiments, he had escaped the commoner kind of pitfalls. He was given to short bursts of lust, and this lust once satisfied, he looked at women impersonally for a while, as one looks at inanimate objects. But at times this lust, usually the result of an inner need and not the outcome of exterior stimulus, would be aroused by the sight of some particular woman. This had been the case with Blondy Belle; she was big, healthy and lascivious. This exactly suited Rico's tastes; she excited him, and for that very reason he was on guard against her.

"Yeah," he said, "I got to lay off Blondy for a while."

She wanted him to come and live with her, but he refused. The offer tickled his vanity, though, for Pepi or Joe Sansone would have jumped at the chance. But not Rico. He fought shy of any kind of ties. A slight relaxing of this principle and you are tangled up before you know it. The strong travel light.

He went out into the living room. Blondy, in a cerise kimono, was pedalling the pianola and singing loudly. The room was in disorder. Stockings hung from the backs of chairs, the dress Blondy had worn the night before was suspended from the chandelier on a coat-hanger, and there was a pile of clothes in the middle of the room.

Blondy turned around and smiled at him, pedalling the piano at the same time.

"What the hell kind of a piece is that?" asked Rico.

"That's an Eyetalian piece," said Blondy. "Ain't it swell?"

"No," said Rico, "I like jazz better."

Blondy stopped the pianola and back-pedalled the roll.

"I got it yesterday because I thought you'd like it," she said.

"Hell, quit kidding," said Rico.

"I sure did. It's from an Opera."

"Yeah? Say, what's wrong with you?"

Blondy looked at him. She had pretensions. Ten years ago she had been a lady's maid and she felt that she was somewhat cultured. One summer she had even made Little Arnie take her to Ravinia Park to hear the Opera. The soprano impressed her by her loud singing; the tenor by his beautiful legs.

"You'd think I was a regular wop to hear you talk," said Rico; "say, I was born in Youngstown and I can't even speak the lingo."

"Well, I guess I wasn't born in the old country either," said Blondy.

She put a new roll on the pianola and Rico sat smoking, while she played it. Rico had no ear for music; he couldn't even whistle, or distinguish one tune from another. But he liked rhythm. There was something straightforward and primitive about jazz rhythms that impressed him.

"That's a good one," he said, when the roll was played through.

"Want to hear some more?"

"No," said Rico, "I got to go."

He rose and went over to the closet for his overcoat, but Blondy said :

"Listen, Rico. I want to see you a minute before you go."

"What about?"

"About Little Arnie."

Rico stared at her.

"What's the idea? To hell with Little Arnie. As long as he's straight with me I ain't got no interest in him at all."

"He ain't straight with nobody."

Rico just looked at her.

Little Arnie had played his hand badly. At first he hadn't minded losing Blondy Belle in the least; she cost him a good deal of money and she bored and irritated him. But he had been kidded unmercifully. As he had no sense of humour whatever and was very touchy in a personal matter, this eventually angered him. In revenge, he talked. He told all who would listen that Blondy Belle was a liar, a crook, and had certain unnatural appetites. Killer Pepi was one of the auditors and he immediately repeated Little Arnie's assertions to his woman, Blue Jay, who ran at once to Blondy Belle. Yes, Little Arnie, who was fifty per cent fool, had played his hand badly.

Blondy lit a cigarette and lay down on the davenport.

"Come over here and sit down," she said; "I'll give you an earful."

"I ain't got no time," said Rico.

Blondy blew out a cloud of smoke.

"What you got on your mind?" said Rico; "spill it."

"All right," said Blondy. "Arnie's giving you a split on the house, ain't he? What's the split?"

"Thirty per cent."

"How do you know you're getting thirty?"

"I look at the books."

Blondy laughed.

"Them books is crooked."

"Straight dope?" asked Rico, his face hardening.

"Sure," said Blondy, "I wasn't gonna say nothing. It wasn't none of my business, but Arnie's been peddling a lot of loose talk about me and I don't take that."

"All right," said Rico, "now you know so damn much, how we gonna prove it?"

"It's a cinch," said Blondy; "hand Arnie's boy, Joe Peeper, some dough and he'll spill the news. Joe hates Arnie."

"Good!" said Rico, banging the table with his fist; "I'll run Arnie out of town and declare you in, Blondy. You got brains."

Blondy looked at him.

"You stick to me, boy, and we'll own the town."

"Don't get swelled up," said Rico, "just because you happened to be in the know."

That's what she liked about Rico. He was hard to impress.

"Hell of a lot of thanks I get for it," said Blondy.

"Don't worry about that," said Rico, his head buzzing with projects, "you'll get something better than thanks."

Rico went to the closet and got his coat and hat.

"Wait a minute, big boy," said Blondy, "you ain't heard it all. Listen, that joint of Arnie's is worth plenty of dough. He ain't gonna give it up without a battle."

"Hell," said Rico, "he's yellow."

"Sure he is. But he's tricky. Rico, if you can't work the Joe Peeper stunt, here's a lever. Remember Limpy John?"

"Sure," said Rico, "they bumped him off."

"Who did?"

"The cops."

Blondy laughed.

"They thought they did. Arnie bumped him off."

Rico grinned.

"I got you."

Rico put on his overcoat.

"Be round tonight?" asked Blondy.

"No, I got business."

"Monkey business."

"No, I got to go cross town. I'll give you a ring tomorrow."

Blondy lay back on the davenport.

"You'll sure be missing something," she said.

"I'll ketch up," said Rico.

When Rico had gone, Blondy played a couple of rolls on the pianola, then she drank half a pint of liquor and went back to bed.

5

Rico found the door of his apartment unlocked. Before entering he unbuttoned his overcoat and took out his automatic. Only one person had a key to his apartment except himself: Otero. If Otero wasn't in there then whoever was in there was in trouble. Rico opened the door slowly. Otero was sitting with his chair tipped back against the wall, smoking a cigarette and dozing.

"Otero!"

Otero opened his eyes.

"Hello, boss."

Rico locked the door behind him.

"Listen, don't you know better than to leave that door open?"

"I forgot, Rico."

Rico took off his overcoat and hat.

"You better keep your head working, boy," said Rico, "or you'll get your neck stretched. What you doing here, anyway?"

Otero got up from his chair and stood dangling his hat.

"I want money."

Rico looked at him.

"I'm broke, boss. I ain't got a cent."

Rico laughed. Otero seemed so helpless.

"You mean to tell me you ain't got a cent out of that Casa Alvarado split?"

Otero shrugged.

"Well, Seal she spends money, spends money. I take it out of my pocket till I ain't got any more." Otero shrugged and rolled a fresh cigarette.

Rico took out his billfold and handed Otero a fifty.

"I'll take that out of your next split."

Otero smiled.

"That's all the same to me, boss."

He was speaking the truth. He hadn't the slightest conception of the value of money. He spent till what he had was gone, then he asked Rico for more. Rico shook his head.

"Listen, Otero, ain't you never gonna get no sense! You got over a grand and a half out of that Casa Alvarado stand. And here you are broke. Why some guys work a whole year for less than that."

Otero shrugged.

"I have worked for two pesos a week."

Rico took some small change out of his pocket and handed it to Otero.

"Go down to the corner and get a couple of *Tribunes*. Get three."

"Three of the same kind?"

"Sure."

Otero went out. Rico opened the window a few inches and sat down beside it. There was a touch of spring in the air and it made him feel restless. He wanted to be doing things. In a week or less, he'd have Little Arnie's big gambling joint. That meant dough and plenty of it. He'd turn it over to Sam Vettori and let him run it. Sam was looking for something to do. Then maybe he could muscle in on the North Side graft. That wasn't easy. Pete Montana was a wise bird and he had the North Side tied up. Well, maybe the Big Boy could help him there. Rico jumped to his feet and began to pace up and down.

Otero came in with the papers. Rico took them from him and tore one of them apart till he came to the magazine section. There it was. Big type proclaimed:

ITALIAN UNDERWORLD CHIEF
GIVEN BIG FEED

Otero, looking over Rico's shoulder, saw the flashlight picture. In his excitement he pushed Rico aside and placing his finger on a section of the picture, cried:

"There I am!"

Rico took the other two papers apart and got out the magazine sections. Then he put the three sections side by side and compared them.

"All too dark," he said.

Nevertheless, having chosen the clearest one of the three, he took his scissors and cut it out.

"I want one too," said Otero.

"All right," said Rico, "help yourself."

6

DeVoss was standing in the lobby when Rico came in. DeVoss looked him over thoroughly, positive that he was out of his element in an atmosphere as exclusive as that of The Bronze Peacock. Not that Rico looked the least bit shabby. If anything, he was dressed more carefully than usual, from his modish derby to his fawn-coloured spats. The big ulster he was wearing hid the loud striped suit and a plain dark muffler hid the loud striped tie. No, sartorially Rico could pass at The Bronze Peacock. But there was something vulgar and predatory about him that did not escape DeVoss.

"That's a bad one there," he told himself.

Rico glanced about the lobby, taking everything in from habit. It was not a good plant but it could be worked. Not that he had any intention of working it, but you never know. He came up to DeVoss and said :

"Excuse me, but where'll I find the manager of this place?"

DeVoss looked at him coldly.

"I'm the manager."

Rico grinned.

"Well," he said, "I guess we got a mutual friend. The Big Boy tells me you and him does business together."

DeVoss's manner changed abruptly.

"Oh, yes. You're one of his friends, are you? What can I do for you?"

"I want to see Joe Massara."

"That's easy," said DeVoss, "he's back in his dressing-room. I'll take you back."

Rico followed DeVoss and they went up a few steps at the end of the lobby and came out into the club proper. It was empty except for a couple of electricians who were working on the stage spotlights.

"So you're one of the Big Boy's friends," said DeVoss, curious.

"I'm Rico."

DeVoss looked at him, startled.

"Oh," he said, "you're Rico."

All the way up the rear corridor DeVoss kept looking sideways at Rico. One of Little Arnie's men had told him about the new Vettori gang chief. Dangerous as dynamite! He congratulated himself on his acumen. By God, he kept repeating to himself, I knew he was a bad one.

DeVoss knocked at Joe's door. Someone called "come in." DeVoss opened the door and Rico followed him into the room. Joe was sitting in his shirt sleeves, his vest off, displaying a pair of fancy suspenders. (Rico made a mental note of the suspenders. His taste ran more to fancy sleeve garters. But if men like Joe were wearing fancy suspenders, why, he'd have to get himself a pair.) Olga Stassoff, in a black, red and gold Japanese kimono was lying on a lounge, holding a Pekinese on her chest and rubbing its face against her own. A big man in evening clothes was standing with his back to the door. When Joe saw Rico he got to his feet in a hurry and stood smiling a little uneasily. The big man turned around.

"Mr. Rico wants to see you, Joe," said DeVoss; then he put his hand on Rico's arm and said: "When you get done with Joe, why, come up to the office and we'll have a little drink."

"Sorry," said Rico, "I don't use it. But thanks just the same."

DeVoss's eyebrows rose.

"You mean you don't drink!"

"Rico drinks milk," said Joe, trying to be funny.

But Rico didn't even smile.

"Yeah," he said, "sometimes I drink milk."

"Well, drop in anyway on your way out," said DeVoss.

DeVoss closed the door. Rico noticed that the girl in the Japanese kimono was staring at him. She didn't look like much to him; too skinny; all the same he insolently ran his eyes over her. The big man said:

"I guess there's no use for us to offer you a drink."

Joe took Rico by the arm.

"Olga, I want you to meet Rico. Rico, this is Olga Stassoff."

"Pleased to meet you," said Rico.

Olga sat up and tried to smile, but it was no use. Rico was repulsive to her, principally because she was certain that he had killed Joe's friend, Tony, but also because he stared at her insolently with his small, pale eyes.

"This boy here," said Joe, taking the big man familiarly by the arm, "is Mr. Willoughby, the millionaire."

"Why bring that up?" said Willoughby.

Rico had an instinctive respect for wealth. Money was power. He smiled affably and offered his hand.

"Pleased to meet you," he said.

Willoughby shook hands strenuously, then he inquired:

"Have you got some private business with Joe?"

"Yeah," said Rico, "but there ain't no hurry about it."

"That's all right," said Willoughby. "Olga and I'll go over next door. Eh, Olga? When you get through, why, give us a rap and we'll come back. Don't suppose I could persuade you to join us in a little supper before the show?"

Rico was flattered.

"Well," he said, "I might."

"Good," said Willoughby; then taking Olga by the hand he pulled her to her feet. But Olga hesitated and stood looking from Joe to Rico.

"Run along, baby," said Joe.

"Well, don't take all night about it," said Olga.

"I won't keep him long," Rico put in.

When Olga and Willoughby had gone Rico said:

"Flying pretty high, ain't you, Joe?"

"Willoughby's just one of Olga's fish. He's gonna back her in a big show."

"Yeah? Well, if that bird's got a million bucks you both better clamp onto him. Nice little Jane you got, Joe."

"Olga's O.K.," said Joe.

Rico unbuttoned his ulster to display his finery. He had on

one of his striped suits. It was dead black with a narrow pink stripe. The colour scheme was further complicated by a pale blue shirt and an orange and white striped tie adorned with the ruby pin.

Joe stared at him.

"All lit up, ain't you, Rico?" he said.

Rico nodded, pleased.

"Yeah, I kind of got it into my head I ought to dress up now."

"They tell me you crowded Sam out," said Joe.

Rico looked at him.

"Didn't nobody tell you the boys was giving a banquet for me?"

"Yeah, they told me," said Joe, hurriedly, "but it was on at the wrong time for me."

Rico took out a cigar and bit off the end of it.

"I ain't seen you since the big stand."

"No," said Joe looking at the floor. "I been laying low. They had me scared."

Rico banged his fist on the arm of his chair.

"Goddam it, Joe, what you got up your sleeve?"

Joe looked startled. He sat silent and from time to time raised his eyes to glance at Rico, who was staring at him.

"Spill it, Joe," said Rico.

"Well," said Joe, "I been making pretty good money with my dancing. Olga and me has got a turn together that's going over big. They want to put us in a show. Listen, Rico, I got enough of the racket. This last stand damn near fixed me. Jesus, but we was lucky."

"We ain't out yet," said Rico, "and we don't want no softies spoiling things."

Rico and Joe stared at each other for a moment. Joe began to get pale.

"You ain't dumb, Joe," said Rico, "what the devil! You mean to tell me you're gonna quit the racket. Why, boy, you ain't seen nothing yet. In a couple of weeks I'm gonna take over Little Arnie's joint. The Big Boy even wants to be declared in. Listen, Joe, you're a smart boy and I can use you. To hell with that dancing stuff. As a front it's O.K., but no man's gonna make his living that way."

Joe slumped down in his chair.

"I got your number, Joe," Rico went on, "it's that damn skirt. She's making a softie of you, Joe."

"Lord, Rico," said Joe, "can't a guy quit? I ain't gonna spill nothing. You think I want to get my neck stretched?"

"Yeah? Look at Tony. He turned soft and they patted him with a spade. Once a guy turns soft he ain't no good in this world. Didn't Humpy get soft on Red Gus and turn State's? Yeah! Who got the neck stretching? Red Gus. Humpy got fifteen years and he'll be out in half of that."

Joe slumped further down in his chair.

"Rico, you know I ain't yellow."

"All right," said Rico, "if that's the dope, I can use you. Ottavio and me has been figuring on a little stand that won't be half bad. I need a good inside man, Joe. A cut will be worth two grand at least."

Someone knocked at the door. It was DeVoss. He came over to Rico and said:

"Mr. Rico, there's a couple of dicks out in the lobby. When I asked them what they wanted, they said they was just looking around."

Rico said:

"Two bits it's Flaherty. All right, Mr. DeVoss, thanks."

DeVoss went out. Joe got to his feet and turned agonized eyes on Rico.

"What did you have to come clear across town for, Rico? Can't you let me alone?"

Rico paid no attention to him.

"There's one Irishman," he said, "that ain't long for this world."

"Rico," said Joe, "for God's sake stay over in your own end of town. I don't want the bulls coming here."

"Listen," said Rico, his eyes glowing, "if I hear any more of this softie stuff I'll only be back once more."

Willoughby and Olga came in.

"Didn't you rap for us?" asked Willoughby.

"No, that was DeVoss," said Rico, "but we're done. Say, Mr. Willoughby, I sure am sorry but I got to pass up that invitation of yours. I got some important business with a couple of guys."

"Sorry," said Willoughby.

"Yes, we're sorry," said Olga, trying to be affable on Joe's account.

Rico shook hands with Joe.

"I'll be seeing you."

"All right, Rico," said Joe.

When Rico emerged he saw DeVoss coming down the corridor. He looked somewhat agitated.

"They're sure enough looking for you, Mr. Rico. For Lord's sake don't cause no trouble in my place."

Rico grinned.

"There won't be no trouble unless them damn dummies out there start it."

Rico followed DeVoss back through the club. On the stage the orchestra was tuning up and a few early couples were sitting at the tables. When they got to the lobby Rico saw Flaherty and another detective. Flaherty came over to him.

"Well, Rico," he said, "kind of out of your territory, ain't you?"

"What the hell of it?"

Rico buttoned his ulster and carefully arranged his muffler.

"Oh, nothing. Don't you remember I told you I was keeping an eye on you? Sure thing. I'm interested in young guys that want to get up in the world."

"Aw, can that," said Rico.

He noticed that people were coming into the place; in the club the orchestra had begun to play. He remembered what the Big Boy had said about DeVoss.

"Let's get the hell out of here," he said, "no use causing DeVoss no trouble. You bulls got about as much regard for a guy as a couple of hyenas."

"You're long on regard yourself, ain't you, Rico?" said Flaherty, laughing.

Rico nodded to DeVoss and went out. Flaherty and the other detective followed him. Rico was standing at the kerb under the canvas marquee. They came up to him. He stared at Flaherty.

"Listen, Flaherty," he said, "did you ever stop to think how you'd look with a lily in your hand?"

"I never did," said Flaherty, with a sneer. "I been at this

game for twenty-five years and I've got better guys than you hung, and I never got a scratch."

Rico took out a cigar and lit it. A taxi drew up at the kerb.

"Well, here's my wagon," said Rico, "want to take a ride?"

"No," said Flaherty, "when we take a ride together I'll have the cuffs on you."

"No Irish bastard'll ever put no cuffs on Rico!"

Flaherty's face got red, but he turned on his heel and was about to go when Rico said:

"And another thing, Flaherty, you was always O.K. with me, see, but now you ain't. You ain't got nothing on me and you ain't got no business trailing me every place I go. Take a tip. Sam and me're getting tired of seeing you guys climb the stairs. The first floor's open to anybody, they even allow cops in there, but the upstairs is private."

"Yeah?" said Flaherty, who had succeeded in controlling his temper.

"Yeah. Some day one of you wise dicks is gonna make a one way trip up them stairs."

"Getting up in the world, ain't you, Rico?" said Flaherty, "maybe you better run for mayor."

Rico slammed the door of the cab. Flaherty turned to the man with him and said:

"I'll gct that swell-headed Dago if it's the last thing I ever do."

PART 5

I

THERE were quite a few wise boys in Little Italy who thought that Rico's sensational rise was a fluke. The matter was talked about a good deal and he was unfavourably compared with Nig Po and Monk De Angelo, former leaders, and there were even those who considered him inferior to Killer Pepi, Ottavio Vettori, and Joe Sansone. This confusion arose because Rico was not understood. He had none of the outward signs of greatness. Neither the great strength and hairiness of Pepi, nor the dash and effrontery of Ottavio Vettori, not the maniacal temper of Joe Sansone. He was small, pale and quiet. In spite of his new finery he wasn't much to look at. He did not swagger, he seldom raised his voice, he never bragged. In other words, the general run of Little Italians could find nothing in him to exaggerate; they could not make a legendary figure of him because the qualities he possessed were qualities they could not comprehend. The only thing that redeemed him in their eyes was his reputation as a killer.

Rico was brave enough, but he did not flaunt his bravery like Kid Bean. Rico was cunning enough, but cunning was not an obsession with him as it was with Sam Vettori. Rico was capable of sudden audacity, but even his audacity had a sort of precision and was entirely without the dash of Ottavio's.

Rico, while he was small and pale, was capable of great endurance, but this endurance of his was nothing compared to Killer Pepi's inhuman vitality. Rico's great strength lay in his single-mindedness, his energy and his self-discipline. The Little Italians could not appreciate qualities so abstract.

The men that were considered his rivals were really not to be compared with him. Killer Pepi was strong and courageous, but he was very erratic and a drug-addict. Ottavio Vettori was daring enough and cool in a tight place, he could shoot straight and he feared nothing, but he was light-minded, dissipated his energies on all sorts of follies, and ran after every woman that looked at him. Joe Sansone, though brave enough and dependable when it came to a sudden action, was a periodic drunkard, and, generally speaking, nervous and unreliable. Sam Vettori, a good man once, had let his congenital lethargy and his congenital love of trickery overcome him; he had become petty and had entirely lost the initiative which, years ago, had put him at the head of the gang. Now he was not even taken seriously by the men he had once led, and but for Rico's authority, he would have sunken into obscurity.

The case of Sam Vettori was a strange one, without its parallel in gang annals. In Little Italy there is no such thing as abdication unless it is accompanied by flight. The old gang leader who is superseded has two alternatives: flight or death. Sam had escaped both. His growing inability to make decisions had lost him his power, but it had also saved his life. Rico did not consider him dangerous. But that was not all. Rico considered him useful. That saved him from flight. With the proper guidance, Sam Vettori was an asset to any gang. He was wise and he knew the ropes.

Sam was docile; not that his hatred for Rico had abated; but things were breaking good, money was rolling in, and Sam loved money above all things. The Vettori gang had never known such prosperity before. Sam was quick to see where his advantage lay. Rico could be killed. Scabby, who hated Rico for some fancied slight and who, for this reason, was faithful to Sam, would have done it. But what would have been the good of that? Sam knew that he was through as a gang leader. With Rico dead, there would be a mad scramble for leadership. Besides, Rico had the devil's own luck, and Scabby might fail. If he failed, Scabby's life and his own wouldn't be worth a plugged dime. No, Sam Vettori accepted a somewhat odd situation philosophically and prospered.

2

Blondy Belle lolled back in her chair and put her fat hands on the table. Rico sat opposite her with his hat tilted over his eyes.

"Well," said Blondy Belle, "I guess that's it, ain't it, Rico?"

Rico nodded.

"I told you not to give that bird a chance. He thinks you're soft."

Rico smiled and twisted his diamond ring round and round.

"He raised the split to fifty per cent, and the books were straight."

"Well," said Blondy, "he couldn't stand prosperity. Listen, you're gonna let him have it, ain't you?"

Blondy hated Little Arnie so that she couldn't sleep at night. She couldn't understand Rico's lenience.

"No," said Rico.

"Hell," said Blondy, "you're getting soft."

"Aw, can that," said Rico; "you want me to get my neck stretched over a dirty double-crosser that ain't worth a good bullet? Listen, I'm gonna run that bird out of town."

Blondy was disgusted. She started to get to her feet, but Rico reached across the table and pushed her back into her chair.

"Sit down," he said, "and cut the funny stuff. If you women ain't awful! Use your head, that's what you got it for."

Blondy sulked. Across the room the orchestra started up and couples crowded out into the roped-off dance floor.

"Don't they ever get sick of dancing?" said Blondy, in a bad temper.

Rico got to his feet.

"Listen," he said, "get yourself a cab and beat it. Go

home and take some aspirin and hit the hay. If you'd lay off that bad liquor you wouldn't always be beefing."

Blondy looked at Rico for a moment, then she said:

"Aw, sit down, Rico. I'll snap out of it."

"No," said Rico, "I got business to look after and I'm getting sick of this beefing. See, I'm getting sick. Any more of this kind of stuff and I'm gonna get me another woman. Hell, I might as well talk to Flaherty as you."

Blondy got to her feet without speaking. Rico never kidded; he meant what he said. Blondy was not used to men like Rico. She often wondered why it was she couldn't seem to get any hold on him.

Silently they walked around the little, roped-off dance floor. Rico told one of the waiters to get him a cab, then, to pass the time, he started putting nickels in a slot machine. After the third nickel, the bell rang and Rico won fifty cents; on the sixth nickel he won again.

"Ain't that good!" said Rico.

He called the man behind the counter.

"Say," he said, "have you seen anybody fooling with this machine?"

The man nodded.

"Yes, sir," he said, "I seen Ottavio doing something to it."

Rico laughed.

"Can you beat that petty crook! He'll be robbing blind men next. Say, tell Sam to get all the machines overhauled. What the hell! He might as well hand out nickels over the counter."

Blondy laughed, glad of this opportunity to put on a change of front.

"Boy, you don't miss anything," she said.

"Well," said Rico, serious, "what's the use of letting somebody gyp you?"

The waiter they had sent for the cab came to tell them that it was outside.

Blondy put her hand on Rico's arm.

"Listen, wise boy," she said, "you got the right dope about that Little Arnie business. Run him out, that's O.K., but do it up brown."

"You watch," said Rico.

He put her in the cab.

"Gonna give me a ring tonight, Rico?" she asked.

"Can't say."

"Well, don't let me ketch you with any more dark hairs on your coat."

"Can that!" said Rico.

Blondy slammed the cab door. Rico stood and watched the cab till it disappeared. Blondy was just like any other woman. Now she had got to the grand rush stage. Always beefing about something. Rico stood looking down the street. It was hot and the city sweltered, but now and then you could feel a breath of lake wind. He looked up at the sky. Stars everywhere.

"It's a swell night," said Rico.

Contrary to custom, he decided to walk down to the newsstand and get a paper. Since his rise, he seldom went out unaccompanied; never at night. Otero, Killer Pepi and Bat Carillo had constituted themselves his bodyguards and one of them was always within calling distance. They were jealous of this privilege and sometimes quarrelled among themselves. But the night tempted Rico; the atmosphere of The Palermo was vile, and the lake breeze was fresh and cool.

He had gone scarcely half a block when a large touring-car with the curtains closed passed him. He saw the car, noticing especially the closed curtains and the fact that the driver was hugging the kerb, and, fearing the worst, he looked about for a shelter, but, as the car passed him and went on, he paid no further attention to it. Stopping in front of a lighted drug-store window he took out his watch and looked at it. One o'clock! Kid Bean and the Killer ought to be back any minute now. Suddenly he looked up. The big touring-car had turned and was coming back at full speed with its exhaust roaring. Rico cursed himself for his carelessness and reached under his armpit for his gun. But the car was abreast of him now and three guns blazed. Rico felt a searing pain in his shoulder and fell to the ground. His gun was stuck in its holster and he couldn't get it out. One of the men leaned out of the car and emptied his gun at Rico, who, helpless on the ground, heard the bullets ring.

"A goddamn fine shot you are!" said Rico.

The big touring-car turned a corner and disappeared. Rico

got to his feet and walked into the drugstore. The screen-door banged behind him and the clerk, who had been lying down behind the counter, got unsteadily to his feet.

"My God," he stammered, "what was all the popping for?"

Then he noticed that there was a torn place on the shoulder of Rico's coat.

"Was they after you, mister?" he asked.

"Yeah," said Rico, "I got brushed. Give me a roll of bandages."

The clerk stood there with his mouth open. People began to come into the store. Some of them knew who Rico was and stood staring at him.

"They put a bullet through my window," said the clerk.

"Listen," said Rico, "go get me a package of bandages."

The clerk finally came to himself and went for the bandages. A crowd had gathered in the street and now there were so many people in the drugstore that the people on the outside couldn't get in. Rico stood with his back to the counter, watching. Blood had begun to drip from his coatsleeve. Before the clerk returned with the bandages, Jastrow, the famous Little Italy cop, pushed his way through the crowd, followed almost immediately by Joe Massara.

"Well," said Jastrow, "somebody finally put one in you, did they, Rico?"

"Yeah," said Rico.

Joe Massara came over and put his hand on Rico's arm. Joe's face was white.

"Hurt you much, boss?"

"No," said Rico, "what the hell you doing way over here?"

"I got tipped off," said Joe. "I couldn't get you on the phone and I began to get nervous. We'd've made it only my cab driver got hooked for speeding."

"Who gave you the tip?" Jastrow demanded.

"Go press the bricks," said Rico, "this ain't your funeral."

Jastrow laughed.

"Rico," he said, "don't you know that the Old Man's taken an awful interest in you?"

"Well, tell him the cops couldn't get me no other way so they hired a couple of gunmen."

Joe laughed. Jastrow laughed also and taking out his notebook began to write in it. The clerk came with the bandages. Joe took them from him and paid him. Before they could get started, Killer Pepi and Otero came shoving their way through the crowd.

"Hello, boys," said Jastrow, looking up from his little book, "your boss got nudged by a hunk of lead."

"So they tell me," said the Killer.

Rico said :

"Let's get the hell out of here."

Jastrow went in front, clearing the way, followed by Otero and Killer Pepi, who had Rico between them. Joe brought up the rear. People were lined to the car-tracks; lights blazed in all the houses along the street, and men hung from the lamp-posts. When they came out of the store, the crowd was so thick that they were unable to get any farther. Jastrow took out his nightstick and flourished it, but the sight of it was enough, the crowd made a path.

As they walked along Joe came up close to Rico and whispered :

"Little Arnie."

Rico nodded. Pepi heard Joe.

"Yeah," he said, "and I'm gonna plug him tonight."

"There won't be no plugging," said Rico.

"Aw, hell," said Pepi.

Otero was excited.

"Yes, yes, Rico," he cried.

"Shut up, you birds," said Rico; "who the hell's running this show?"

A crowd was waiting for them in front of The Palermo. Bat Carillo and Ottavio Vettori began to yell as soon as they saw that Rico was on his feet.

Jastrow turned around.

"Well, I guess I done my duty."

"Sure," said Rico, "come and have a drink."

"Nothing doing," said Jastrow, then he shouted : "You birds quit your damn yelling and get in off the sidewalk."

Everybody laughed. They all liked Jastrow, who had the reputation of being on the square. Rico went in escorted by a mob of Little Italians. In the club people were standing on the tables; the orchestra was playing loudly; and Sam

Vettori, in the middle of the deserted dance floor, was waving his arms wildly and bellowing.

When they saw Rico there was a tumult.

"Rico! Rico! Rico!"

Killer Pepi and Otero, intoxicated by the excitement, grabbed each other and began to dance. Joe waved the bandages. Rico took off his hat and smiled.

On the way up the stairs Rico turned to Joe and said:

"Go get The Sheeny."

Killer Pepi took Rico by the arm.

"He's upstairs now, boss," he said: "the Kid got plugged."

"How'd you make out?" Rico inquired.

"O.K.," said Killer Pepi; "we was making a get-away on the third stand when one of the guys plugged the Kid. He ain't hurt much. Just skinned him."

Killer Pepi and Kid Bean had robbed twenty-five filling-stations in the last two weeks.

"All right," said Rico, "you guys have been on the up and up. Split the money two ways."

"That's the talk, boss," said the Killer.

Otero knocked on the door. Joe Sansone's face appeared at the grating, then the door swung open.

The Sheeny was working on Kid Bean. The Kid was lying on the card table, smoking a cigarette. His shirt was off and there was a smear of blood on his hairy chest. When he saw Rico he said:

"They damn near hit the target, boss."

He pointed to a pierced heart tattooed on his chest. He was as proud of his tattooing as a Maori chief.

"The boss got plugged," said Pepi.

"What!" yelled the Kid, sitting up; "go fix him up, Sheeny."

He gave The Sheeny a push. But Rico said:

"Finish up the Kid first. I can wait."

"Only jist got to bandage him yet," said The Sheeny with his ingratiating smile.

The Sheeny was a graduate doctor, but he had been sent up for an illegal operation and his licence had been revoked. He said his name was Lazarro, but nobody believed him and everybody referred to him simply as The Sheeny.

Rico took off his coat and shirt, and sat waiting. His wound had stopped bleeding.

Joe Massara came over and stood by his chair. Joe's big cut for an inside job had pulled him back to the fold. He never talked any more about quitting the racket. The Courtney affair had blown over apparently, and he had regained his confidence.

"Joe," said Rico, "how come they gave you the tip?"

"Well," said Joe, "I ain't sure, but I think it was an outsider that didn't know nobody but me. He sure had the dope all right. He said the guys were gonna park at twelve. They didn't expect you out till two or three."

"A fine bunch of gunmen Arnie picked!"

"Yeah," said Joe.

The Kid climbed off the table and stood feeling his chest.

"Boy, I thought I was plugged for sure."

"They just bounce off you," said Pepi.

The Sheeny began to bathe Rico's wound.

" 'Tain't much," he said, "but it pays to be careful."

When The Sheeny had got Rico bandaged, Rico put on his shirt and sat smoking. Bat Carillo and Ottavio Vettori, whom he had sent for, came in and sat down beside him. The Sheeny put on his hat.

"Well," he said, smiling at Rico, "I guess I'm done. If you guys have any trouble with them wounds let me know."

Rico got his billfold and gave The Sheeny a fifty.

"Thank you! Thank you!" said The Sheeny, bowing.

Joe Sansone let him out.

Rico said:

"Now, listen, you birds, tonight's the big clean-up. If these guys want trouble, why, that's just what we're looking for."

"You bet," said Killer Pepi.

"Now," Rico went on, "I got things fixed with Joe Peeper and I'm gonna to give Little Arnie the grand rush right away. I want Killer Pepi and Otero and Ottavio to go with me."

"How about me?" demanded Joe Sansone.

"You too, Joe. And you, Bat, I want you to take your gang and smash up Jew Mike's. Run everybody out and then smash the place. If Little Arnie wants trouble, why that's what we got the most of. Got it?"

"O.K.," said Bat, "how about the rods?"

"Don't use 'em," said Rico; "Jew Mike's yellow and he won't put up no fight."

"Them guys of mine sure are hard to hold on to," said Carillo, grinning.

"That's your job," said Rico. "We got to watch this plugging stuff with Flaherty on our trail."

"O.K., boss," said Carillo.

3

WHEN the doorman saw Rico get out of the automobile he stood stunned, then, pulling himself together, he made an attempt to run. But Pepi crossed the pavement in two strides, grabbed him by the collar and pushed him ahead of him up the stairs.

"Listen, Handsome," said Pepi, "you tell the look-out we're O.K. or they'll bury you."

At the head of the stairs the doorman spoke to the look-out through the shutter.

"These birds are all right," he said.

The look-out opened the door and Pepi shoved a gun against him.

"Turn your back, Buddy," said Pepi, "and march straight ahead of me."

Rico, followed by Joe Sansone, Ottavio Vettori, and Otero, climbed the long flight of stairs and entered the lobby. The lobby was deserted except for two or three couples. Beyond it, through a big arched doorway, they could see the crowded roulette wheels. Rico caught up with Pepi and said to the doorman :

"Where's Joe Peeper?"

The doorman had an agonized look. He was sure they were going to kill him. He just stood there, unable to force himself to speak.

"Say," said Pepi, "speak up."

The doorman pointed to the door.

"He's in with the boss, is he?" said Rico.

The doorman nodded.

"Yeah," said the look-out, eager to get in good, "Joe's in there with the boss and a couple of other guys."

"All right," said Rico, "now, Pepi, if the door's locked, do your stuff."

Pepi could force the heaviest door with his shoulder.

Joe Sansone tried the door; it was locked.

"Now," said Rico, "Pepi'll force the door. You cover him, Joe, in case somebody in there gets nervous and pulls a gat. I'll follow you. Otero, you stay out here and don't let nobody in. You watch this pair of hard guys here, Ottavio." Rico jerked his thumb toward the look-out and the doorman.

"You don't have to watch us," said the doorman.

They all laughed.

"All right, Pepi," said Rico.

Pepi hunched his shoulders and flung himself against the door. It opened with a crash. They saw four startled men rise half way out of their chairs and stand staring. Joe Peeper cried:

"It's Rico!"

Pepi was on his hands and knees in the middle of the room, but Joe Sansone stepped in behind him and covered the four men with his big automatic. Rico came in, took off his hat and bowed.

"Hello, Arnie," he said; "how's business?"

Little Arnie sat with his mouth slightly open. As a rule Little Arnie was imperturbable. He hid an excess of both cunning and timidity behind a cold, repellent, sallow Jewish mask. But this cyclonic entry was too much for him. His mask had slipped, revealing a pale, terrified countenance.

"Well," he said, "what's the game?"

Joe Peeper, who was in Rico's pay, said:

"Pull up a chair, you guys."

Pepi found two chairs. Joe Sansone and Rico sat down; Pepi stood behind Rico's chair.

Little Arnie turned to the two men sitting beside him. They were strangers to Rico and they looked tough.

"I don't know what this is all about," said Arnie, "but it's a private row, so you guys better beat it."
Rico said very quietly :
"Nobody's gonna leave this room."
One of the toughs shouted :
"Think not, wop ! Well, who the hell's gonna stop us."
Before Rico could reply, Joe Sansone said :
"Me, I'm gonna stop you, see ! And I ain't gentle. I'm just itching to put some lead in a couple of hard guys."
"Yeah," said Rico, smiling, "you guys are invited to this private party."
The two men looked at Arnie, who sat tapping his desk with a pencil.
"Say," said one, "you sure got a fine bunch of friends, Arnie."
"Yeah," said Arnie.
Pepi laughed and said :
"Yeah, he sure has. Arnie, you ought to had better sense than to get a couple of outside yaps to bump Rico off."
Nobody said anything. Arnie took out a cigar and lit it. The two strangers sat staring at Rico. Pepi sat staring at them. Finally he asked :
"Where you guys from?"
The men looked uneasily at Arnie. Little by little they were losing their nerve.
"Speak up," said Pepi, "where you guys from?"
"We're from Detroit," said one of the men.
"Where the hell's that?" Joe Sansone inquired. "I never heard of it."
"Say," said Pepi, "don't you know that tough guys like you oughtn't to be running around loose. No sir. You're liable to get arrested for firing a rod in the city limits."
"Listen," said one of the men from Detroit, "what you guys got against us? We ain't done nothing. We just got in."
They were thoroughly intimidated.
Arnie, who had recovered his poise, said :
"Well, Rico, what's the talk? Let's have it."
Pepi and Joe Sansone both started to talk at once, but Rico motioned for them to be quiet.
"Arnie," said Rico, "you're through. If you ain't out of town

by tomorrow morning, you won't never leave town except in a box."

Arnie said nothing but sat staring at the smoke rising from his cigar.

"In the first place," Rico went on, "you been double-crossing me for two months. In the second place you hire these bums here to pop me. Now I guess that's about all."

Arnie laughed.

"Rico," he said, "somebody has sure been stringing you. Why, you ought to know I wouldn't double-cross you. Hell, that wouldn't help me none."

"Can that," said Rico. "Your number's up, Jew. Take it like a man."

Arnie's face got red.

"Listen, Rico, if you think you can muscle into this joint you're off your nut."

"All right, Joe," said Rico, jerking his head in Joe Peeper's direction, "spill it."

Joe Peeper looked sideways at Arnie.

"The books're crooked, Rico," said Joe Peeper; "he's been gypping you out of half your split every week."

The Detroit toughs began to shift about uneasily.

"Well, you two-timing bastard," said Arnie.

Rico laughed.

"Arnie," he said, "that's that. Here's the dope. You get your hat and beat it. Leave the burg. If I ever hear about you being in town again, why, I'm gonna turn the Killer loose on you."

"Yeah," said Pepi, "and I never did like kikes."

"I ain't any too fond of them, myself," said Joe Sansone.

Arnie meditated. Rico said :

"I been square with you, Arnie, but you couldn't stand prosperity, that's all. So take it standing up."

"What the hell else can he do?" Pepi demanded.

"I'll tell you what I can do," said Arnie, "I can have a talk with Mr. Flaherty."

Arnie studied Rico carefully to see what effect this would have. But Rico merely smiled at him.

"Getting pretty low, Arnie," he said, "when you take the bulls in with you." Then he paused and leaned forward in his chair. "If you go to see Mr. Flaherty you better have an alibi because he might ask you about Limpy John."

Arnie dropped his cigar and sat staring into space, his hands lying palms up on the table.

"All over but the shouting," said Joe Sansone, "somebody better throw in a towel. But I don't suppose the dirty bums in Detroit ever heard of towels."

"Aw, lay off of us," said one of the Detroit toughs.

Joe Sansone stared at him.

"Say, Gyp-the-Blood, I bet they think you're a pretty hard bird where you live, don't they?"

Arnie turned to Joe Peeper.

"Well, Joe," he said, "you sure put the skids under me."

"Sure I did," said Joe Peeper; "you thought you could bat me around and make me like it."

Pepi laughed.

"Arnie," he said, "you better go back to Detroit with your boy friends."

When Rico and his men left Arnie's joint Joe Peeper followed them. As soon as they reached the pavement, Joe walked up to Rico and said :

"You sore at me, Rico?"

All Rico's men stopped and stood staring at Joe, wondering what his game was.

"You guys get in the car," said Rico.

They all got in except Pepi, who stood with his back against the car, his right hand in his pocket. Pepi didn't trust anybody who had ever been mixed up with Little Arnie.

"What's on your mind, Joe?" Rico demanded.

"I thought you acted like you was sore at me," said Joe Peeper; "honest to God, Rico, I didn't know nothing about them Detroit bums. I didn't know what Arnie was up to. Lord, you know I wouldn't double-cross you after all you done for me."

"Well, who said you did?"

"Nobody," said Joe, "only it looked funny, and I thought maybe you guys had got a wrong notion. I'd be a sap to pull anything like that."

Rico laughed.

"Forget it," he said.

Rico started to get into the automobile, but Joe took hold of his arm.

"How about me, Rico?" he said. "If I stick around here they'll bump me off sure."

"Yeah?" said Rico; "say, them guys wouldn't bump nobody off now. But get in. I can use you, Joe."

Joe got in the back seat with Otero and Ottavio Vettori. He talked to them all the way back to The Palermo, trying to get in good with them but they said nothing.

4

The next day in the society column of one of the Chicago papers there appeared a small item, which read:

"Mr. Arnold Worch, of the North Side, has just left for Detroit where he intends to spend the summer. He was accompanied by two of his Detroit friends, who have been in Chicago for a short stay."

This was the work of Ottavio Vettori. The underworld was convulsed and thousands of extra copies of the paper were sold. The clipping was to be found pasted up in all the barrooms, gambling joints, and dance-halls. Rico and Ottavio Vettori had become famous overnight.

Little Arnie wasn't the only one who left town. Several of Little Arnie's henchmen, who had been closely connected with the attempted killing, followed him into exile. Joseph Pavlovsky, the doorman, who had driven the car, went to Hammond, where, on the money Arnie had given him, he opened a speak-easy. Pippy Coke, who with the two Detroit gunmen had done the shooting, went with Pavlovsky, and they were followed by two croupiers, who had shadowed Rico.

Arnie's gang was smashed and the Little Italians took over a territory they hadn't controlled since the days of Monk De Angelo.

Arnie had come to Chicago from New York about five years ago. His reputation had got so bad in New York that no one would do business with him. He came west with a small stake and was lucky enough to arrive at just the right time. Kips Berger, also formerly of New York and once one of Arnie's pals, had gone broke and was willing to sell out his big gambling joint for practically nothing. Arnie bought it and prospered. This gambling joint was in a neutral zone, touching Little Italy on the south and the vast territory that Pete Montana controlled on the north. Arnie was acute enough to see his advantage. He worked hard at his job and in a little while had consolidated his territory. But he was not a good chief: first, because he was a coward, second, because his closest associate couldn't trust him, third, because he was inclined to lose his head in an emergency. His lieutenant, Jew Mike, was a tougher and more violent replica of his chief. Between them they bossed the territory, but under them the gang never prospered and their hold was at best precarious. They held on only because there was little or no opposition. Their gangsters were a poor lot and were content to take small splits. On the south, Sam Vettori was slipping and his lethargy prevented him interfering; on the north the great Pete Montana was magnificently indifferent.

Arnie had been slipping for the last year or so, and Rico's sudden rise had accelerated his decline. Arnie, fearing the worst, committed blunder after blunder; first, he made advances to Rico, then, getting Rico's protection for a thirty per cent split, things looked too easy and he began to double-cross him. Lastly, although he should have known better, he made the tactical error of trying to get Rico killed. If he had succeeded his position would not have been improved; he would have been worse off, because the Vettori gang would have made short work of him.

No one regretted the passing of Little Arnie. He had never been straight with anybody. No one could depend on him and he had none of the qualities that go to make up a good gang chief. The wonder is that he lasted as long as he did.

Arnie's fall was the signal for a series of minor tumbles. Jew Mike, whose joint Bat Carillo and his gang had demolished, fled to the South Side, where he opened a couple of vice-joints. Kid Burg moved to Cicero, and Squint Maschke, after a short exile, offered his services to Rico, who gave him twenty-four hours to make a second disappearance. With the fall of Arnie's three lieutenants, the last vestiges of his rule vanished.

5

Otero helped Rico out of his coat, then, while Rico doused his face at the wash stand, he sat down, tipped back his chair and rolled himself a cigarette.

"You better lay down, Rico, and get some rest," said Otero; "you ain't looking so good."

"I'm O.K.," said Rico.

But this was bravado. He had slept only four hours in the last two days; his face was pale and drawn and he suffered from an intermittent fever. His wound, though a slight one, was not healing properly, and The Sheeny had warned him that he had better take it easy. Inactivity at any time was abhorrent to Rico; now it was impossible. His big chance had come. Nothing could stop him now but a hunk of lead in the right spot.

Rico, a little unsteady on his legs, stood staring at Otero.

"You're sure making yourself at home," he said.

"Well," said Otero, "I think I stay."

Rico laughed.

"Listen, I don't need no nurse. Beat it."

"No," said Otero, tossing away his cigarette and starting to roll another one, "I think I stay."

Rico walked over to the bed and stood staring at it. If he had been alone he would have flopped down and been asleep in an instant.

"Think I'll catch a little sleep," he said; "you beat it, Otero."

Otero didn't say anything. He finished rolling his cigarette, lit it, and tipped his hat down over his eyes.

"Goddamn it," cried Rico, "beat it! I'm sick of you trailing me like a Chicago Avenue bull. I ain't gonna drop in my tracks."

"All right," said Otero, "you lay down. I finish my cigarette."

Rico threw himself on the bed, fully dressed except for his coat. He put his hands under his head and tried to keep awake by staring at the ceiling. But in a moment he was asleep.

Otero sat looking at his chief. All along he'd known. Rico was a great man like Pancho Villa. Even in Toledo when he and Rico were sticking up filling-stations, he knew. A little, skinny young fellow with a little mustache, sure, that's what everybody saw. But everybody didn't have the eyes of Otero.

Otero flung his second cigarette on the floor and rolled another one. Rico turned from side to side in his sleep and mumbled. His face was white and drawn. Otero got to his feet and went over to look at him. No, Rico was not well. Otero put his hand on Rico's forehead. Fever! He stood looking down at his chief, shaking his head.

"Like hell!" cried Rico; "you can't hand Rico none of that bunk. No Irish bastard'll ever put no cuffs on Rico."

Otero went back to his chair and sat dozing under his big hat, while Rico tossed from side to side and talked.

Someone knocked at the door. Otero was slow in opening his eyes, but Rico sat up, stared for a moment, then jumped out of bed and got his automatic.

"Go see who it is," he said to Otero; "don't open the door. Ask them."

Otero went over to the door and called:

"Who's there?"

There was a short silence, then a voice with a marked Italian accent said:

"A couple of right guys. We want to see Rico."

Otero turned and looked at Rico, who came over to the door.

"Listen, you right guys," said Rico, "I'll give you a one-two-three to get out of the hall and then I'm gonna start pumping lead. Got it?"

There was a pause.

"Rico," said another voice, a deeper voice with no trace of

an accent, "you don't know me, but I'm Pete Montana and I want to talk turkey."

Otero and Rico exchanged a stupefied look.

"Pete," said Rico, "do you know the Big Boy?"

"Sure."

"What's his name in full?"

"James Michael O'Doul."

"All right, Otero," said Rico, "let 'em in."

Otero unbarred the door. Rico, with his gun still levelled, stood a little behind the door, watching.

Pete Montana, followed by Ritz Colonna, his lieutenant, came in. Montana, in private life Pietro Fontano, was a big, solemn, respectable-looking Italian. He was dressed very quietly, wore no jewellery, and carried a cane. Colonna, once a ham prize-fighter, was a small, bull-necked man with a battered, dark face. His clothes were shabby and he wore an old cap on the side of his head.

Montana and Rico stood measuring each other. Rico looked small and frail beside the robust Montana, but Rico wasn't impressed, for Montana looked fat and puffy, like Sam Vettori. Otero barred the door.

"Get a couple of chairs, Otero," said Rico.

Otero dragged up the only two chairs in the room and Montana and Colonna sat down. Otero squatted on his heels with his back to the wall and Rico sat on the bed.

Montana took out a monogrammed cigar-case and passed it around, then he selected one of the cigars himself and cut off the end with a little gold cutter on his watch chain.

"Mopping up, ain't you, Rico?" asked Montana, who kept his eyes lowered.

"Well," said Rico, "Arnie was double-crossing me."

"He wasn't no good," said Colonna; "I was just aching to bump that bird off."

Montana motioned for him to be quiet.

"They slung some lead, didn't they, Rico?"

"Yeah, and I stopped some of it. Nothing to shout about."

"If he'd've got you, his number was up," said Montana, "you know, I been watching you ever since you muscled in on Sam Vettori."

"Sure thing. We been taking an interest in you, ain't we, Ritz?"

"Yeah?"

Ritz grinned.

"That's the word," he said.

"Sure," said Montana, "you're on the up and up with us."

"Well," said Rico, "that's O.K. with me."

Montana looked up at Rico suddenly.

"Any guy that can muscle in on Sam Vettori and Little Arnie is on the up and up with me. The Big Boy's with me there."

Rico smoked and said nothing. But he wondered what the game was. Was Pete Montana getting soft like Sam Vettori? Could it be possible that the great Pete Montana was turning sap? All his palaver and softie talk. Rico's head began to buzz.

"Look," said Montana, "I used to work Arnie's territory myself, but it slowed down, you know what I mean. It wasn't worth nothing when Kips Berger had it, and after Arnie got it I didn't pay no attention. I got all I can handle, ain't I, Ritz?"

"That's the word," said Ritz.

"Yeah," said Montana, "by rights that territory's mine, get the idea? I could get all the protection I wanted, but I don't muscle in on no right guy, see? Kiketown's yours, Rico."

"Much obliged," said Rico; "I ain't looking for no trouble with you, Pete."

"That's the talk," said Montana; then he turned to Ritz: "see, Ritz, you had the wrong steer."

"Yeah, I had the wrong steer," said Ritz.

Montana turned back to Rico.

"Yeah," he said, "some wise guys was giving Ritz a lot of bull. Ritz said you was trying to muscle in on my territory."

Rico thought he was dreaming. So this was the great Pete Montana. A guy that couldn't turn over in bed without getting plastered all over the front page. All that softie stuff was a front. Pete Montana was scared.

"No," said Rico, "them guys don't know what they're talking about."

Montana smiled blandly.

"Maybe we can team up on a job or two, Rico. I like your work. The Big Boy's no fool and he thinks you're the goods. Yeah, maybe we can team up, but I ain't making no promises. Only this. I ain't looking for no split on Arnie's lay-out. She's yours."

"Don't forget the hide-out, chief," said Ritz.

Montana smiled again.

"By God, I sure enough did forget it. Yeah, Rico, some of Ritz's boys has got a hide-out a half a block from Arnie's joint. That's O.K., ain't it?"

Rico's manner changed. He lost his affability and his face became serious.

"Well," he said, "as long as there ain't no cutting in. I won't stand for no cutting in."

Montana looked at Ritz. Ritz said :

"Hell, there won't be no cutting in."

"What do you say, Pete?" asked Rico.

Montana meditated, pulling at one of his thick lips. Otero sat watching Rico. Caramba! Here was little Rico telling the big Pete Montana where to get off. Otero never took his eyes off Rico's face.

"Well," said Montana, "they're my men and I'm behind them. If there's any cutting in, why, I'll settle with you, Rico. Christ, no use for us to fight over a little thing like that. Anyway, if we get along, I'll put you in on the alcohol racket."

"All right," said Rico, "you and me can do business, Pete."

Montana got up and offered Rico his hand. They pumped arms briefly. Then Pete said :

"Well, I guess we'll saunter. But let me give you a tip, Rico. You're getting too much notice, get the idea? You got the bulls watching you. I know a new guy has always got to expect that, but take it easy for a while. They'll go to sleep; they always do."

Rico admired Montana's shiftiness, but he wasn't fooled. Pete was trying to tie him up, make him leery.

"Much obliged," said Rico; "a new guy has got a lot to learn."

Montana smiled blandly, certain he had scored.

"Well," said Montana, "so long. Maybe I'll drop down to your new joint and give it the once over some night."

"All right," said Rico, "just let me know."

Otero unbarred the door. Montana started out; Ritz offered his hand to Rico, then followed his chief. Otero barred the door.

Rico stood in the middle of the room, staring into space. Otero said :

"He ain't so much."

Rico laughed out loud.

"Otero," he cried, "you said a mouthful."

PART 6

I

RICO felt small and unimportant in the Big Boy's apartment. He was intensely self-centered and as a rule surroundings made no impression on him. But he had never seen anything like this before. He sat in the big, panelled dining-room, eating cautiously, dropping his fork from nervousness, and looking furtively about him. From time to time he pulled at his high, stiff collar, and when he caught the Big Boy's eye he grinned.

Joe Sansone had dressed him so that he would look presentable. It had taken a good deal of management and tact, but Joe Sansone was a stickler for clothes and persevered with Rico, who swore at him at first and wouldn't listen.

"Look, boss," he said, "you're getting up in the world. Ain't none of us ever been asked to eat with the Big Boy at his dump. Hear what I'm telling you. Nobody's ever crashed the gates before but Pete Montana. See what I mean? You don't want the Big Boy to think you ain't got no class."

Joe had his own dress suit cleaned and pressed, and punctually at five he presented himself at Rico's door with the outfit under his arm. Rico had resisted from the beginning; first, he balked at the suspenders, then the starched shirts. Joe, labouring with the studs, the buttoned shoes, the invincible collar, cursed and sweated. Rico resisted. But Joe won.

As Joe was ten pounds heavier than Rico, the dress suit was not precisely a perfect fit, but as Joe said "men are wearing their clothes a lot looser now." To which Rico sardonically replied: "Yeah? Say, they rig you up better than this in stir."

Finally Joe got Rico into his harness. Rico stamped about declaring that he'd be goddamned if he'd go out looking like that. Why, the Big Boy would think he was off his nut.

"You look fine, boss," said Joe.

"Yeah," said Rico, "all I need is a napkin over my arm."

But Joe moved Rico's bureau out from its corner and tipped the mirror so Rico could get a full length view of himself. He was won over immediately. Why, honest to God, he looked like one of them rich clubmen he read about in the magazines. The enormous white shirtfront, the black silk coat lapels, the neatly-tied white tie dazzled him.

"I guess I don't look so bad," he said to Joe; "we got plenty of time, let's go down to Sam's place for a while."

Rico played with his dessert and looked about the room. The Big Boy ate with gusto, smacking his lips. The magnificence of the Big Boy's apartment crushed Rico. He stared at the big pictures of old time guys in their gold frames; at the silver and glass ware on the serving table; at the high, carved chairs. Lord, why, it was like a hop dream.

He shook his head slowly.

"Yeah," said the Big Boy, glancing negligently about him, "and I sure paid for it. See that picture over there?" He pointed to an imitation Valesquez. "That baby set me back one hundred and fifty berries."

Rico stared.

"Jesus, one hundred and fifty berries for a picture!"

"Yeah," said the Big Boy, "but that ain't nothing. See that bunch of junk over there?" He jerked his head in the direction of the serving table. "That stuff set me back one grand."

Rico stared.

"One grand for that stuff?"

"Sure," said the Big Boy, "that's the real thing. Only what the hell, I say! A plate's to eat off, ain't it? What's the odds what it's made of? But I got a spell about two years ago. I had a pot full of money and I thought, well, other guys that ain't got as much dough as I got put on a front, so why shouldn't I? Sure, I could buy and sell guys that's got three homes and a couple of chuckwagons. So I got a guy down at a big store, you know, one of them decorators, to pick me out a swell apartment and fix it up A-1. So he did. I got a library too and a lot of other stuff that ain't worth a damn. I was talking to a rich guy the other day and he said

I was a damn fool to buy real books because he had a library twice as big as mine and dummy books. What the hell! If a guy's gonna have a library, why, I say do it right. So there you are. I got so damn many books it gives me a headache just to look at 'em through the glass. Shakespeare and all that stuff."

"Yeah?" said Rico, stupefied.

A servant took away their dessert and brought coffee. Then he passed a humidor full of cigars. Rico took one of the fat, black cigars, lit it, and tipped his chair back. What a way to live!

"Yeah," said the Big Boy, "I got a lot of dough tied up in this dump. I get rent free, though. Eschelman, the contractor, owns this dump and he knows how I stand in the city. Boy, he puts up what he pleases and gets away with it. See the idea, Rico? If a guy stands in with me, he owns the burg."

"Sure," said Rico, "you're a big guy."

"I get him contracts, too," said the Big Guy; "course I get mine out of it, but I made that guy. When he came here from down state he didn't have an extra pair of pants, now he's climbing. Yeah, if I had a wife and a couple of kids, why, I'd build me a big house out in some swell suburb, but as it is, I'd just as leave be here on one floor. I got everything I need and then some."

"Sure," said Rico.

"Let's go in the library," said the Big Boy, "it's more comfortable in there."

The Big Boy told the servant to take their coffee into the library. Then he got up and Rico followed him. Then Big Boy put his hand on Rico's shoulder.

"Kind of lit up yourself tonight, ain't you, Rico?"

"Yeah, I thought I better put on the monkey suit."

"That's right, Rico. May as well learn now."

"Sure," said Rico.

The Big Boy motioned Rico to a chair, then sat down. Rico looked about him at the great expanse of glass guarding tier after tier of books. Lord, if a guy'd read that many books he'd sure know a lot!

"Rico," said the Big Boy, "let's talk serious."

"All right," said Rico.

The Big Boy leaned forward in his chair and stared at Rico.

"Listen," he said, "I'm gonna talk and you ain't gonna hear a word I say, see, this is inside dope and if it gets out it'll be just too bad for somebody."

"You know me," said Rico.

"All right," said the Big Boy; "get this: if I didn't think a hell of a lot of you I wouldn't be asking you to eat with me. You're on the square, Rico, and you're a comer, see. You got the nerve and you're a good, sober, steady guy. That's what we need. Trouble with most of these guys they ain't got nothing from the collar up. O.K. Now, listen. Pete Montana's through."

Rico nearly leapt out of his chair.

"Yeah?"

"Now don't get excited," said the Big Boy, "because, when it gets out, there's gonna be hell to pay. Ritz Colonna and a couple of other lowdown bums is gonna make a rush, see, and that means that somebody's gonna get hurt."

"Sure," said Rico, settling back.

"But not you," said the Big Boy; "you're gonna lay back and let them dumb eggs bump each other off, then we'll get our licks in, see? Pete's through. The Old Man's gonna have a talk with him tomorrow or the next day and Pete's gonna mosey. He's all swelled up, thinks he's king and all that stuff, but wait till the Old Man gets through with him. Why, he can hang that guy. Besides that, he can turn the Federal guys loose on him for peddling narcotics. And boy, how he peddles them! He built that big house of his on 'em. Well, see how things are? I can't spill no more."

"Well," said Rico, "I'm on."

"All right," said the Big Boy, "but listen: I'm doing a hell of a lot for you and when I get you planted I want plenty of service."

"You'll sure get it," said Rico.

Rico, with the Big Boy's cigar still between his teeth, lay in the taxi and stared out at the tangle of traffic on Michigan Boulevard. Things were sure to God looking up! Five years ago he wasn't nobody to speak of; just a lonely yegg, sticking up chain-stores and filling-stations. Chiggi had sure given him the right dope. He remembered one night in Toledo when he was pretty low. There was a blonde he used to meet at one of the call-houses and she sure did satisfy him, but, oh boy, she had to have the coin on the nose or there wasn't anything doing. Well, he didn't have a red. He was just sitting there in Chiggi's thinking about the blonde, when Chiggi came over and said: "Listen, kid, you got big town stuff in you. What you want around here? Get somebody to stake you or hit the rods. Hell, don't be a piker." Well, Chiggi staked him, but he blew the stake on the blonde, oh, boy what a couple of days, and then he hit the rods with Otero. Little Italy sure looked good to them. They didn't have a good pair of pants between them, and a bowl of mulligan tasted better than the stuff he'd ate at the Big Boy's. Well, here he was riding taxis and hobnobbing with guys like James O'Doul, who paid one grand for a bunch of crockery. Yeah, here he was!

Rico saw nothing but success in the future. With the Big Boy behind him he couldn't be stopped, and when he once got some place he knew how to stay there. Play square with the guys that are square with you; the hell with everybody else.

Rico smoked his cigar slowly (he had six more of them in his pocket), and looked absently at the jam of traffic: taxis, Hispano-Suizas, Fords, huge double-decked buses, leaning as they turned corners. Rico dropped the cigar butt out the window. Lying back in his seat he observed:

"And I thought Pete Montana was such a hell of a guy!"

2

OLGA was only partly dressed when Joe burst in on her. She looked at him, startled.

"My Lord," she said, "what makes you so pale, Joe?"

"Got any liquor?" demanded Joe.

Olga opened a drawer and handed him a flask. He tipped it up and took a long pull, then he stood with the flask in his hand staring at the wall.

"Joe," Olga insisted, "what's wrong with you?"

Joe came to himself, screwed the top on the flask, and handed it back to Olga.

"Boy, I got a shock," said Joe.

Olga came over and put her arm around him.

"Tell Olga all about it."

"Well," said Joe, "I was finishing up my Pierrot dance, see, and you know when it's dark and they got the spot on you you can't see nothing. Well, I was circling the outside of the floor like I do before I take that last leap when some dame at a corner table gives a yell, a hell of a yell. Sibby hears the yell and switches on all the lights and here I am, right in front of a dame that looks like she's off her nut. She was standing up and she had her hands on the table and she was staring right at me. If I didn't feel funny, boy! Well, there was a guy with her and he kept asking her what was the matter, but she wouldn't say nothing. I thought she was gonna jump right on me, she looked so funny, yeah, that dame sure looked funny."

Joe paused and meditated. Olga laughed.

"Listen," she said, "you better lay off the liquor."

"No, straight," said Joe, "you know I kind of got the idea she recognized me or something, but, hell, I never seen her before. She's an old dame, about forty, and she's got peroxide hair. There was a guy with her, a nice looking guy, and he kept saying, 'What's the matter, Nell, what's the matter, Nell, what's the matter, Nell', but he couldn't get nothing out of her."

Olga laughed again.

"Well, this ain't nothing to write home about," she said. "I thought I was gonna to get a thrill. We better change bootleggers, Joe."

"Aw, lay off," said Joe. "I'm telling you, you'd've got all the kick you're looking for if you'd heard that dame yell."

"Well, what happened?" demanded Olga, who was getting impatient.

Joe got the flask and took another pull at it before he answered her. The colour had come back into his face now and he felt much better.

"Soon as the boss found out there was something wrong he came in and asked this dame if he could do anything for her. And she says, 'Yes, get me a taxi.' The guy with her says, 'What the devil, Nell.' And she says, 'I want to go home.' So they went out. Boy, the way that dame looked at me, like I was, God, I don't know what!"

"Say, listen," said Olga, "you been hitting the pipe?"

"Aw, lay off," said Joe; "that dame got something on her mind, see. She's got something on her mind."

Someone knocked. Olga called "come in" and a waiter opened the door and bowed.

"Mr. Willoughby wants to know if we can bring the table in now, Miss Stassoff."

"Sure," said Olga, "bring it in."

"Yes, ma'am," said the waiter, then he cupped his hands and called down the corridor: "Allez!"

Joe lay down on the lounge and lit a cigarette. Olga went over to her dressing-table, made up her face, and put on her Japanese kimono.

Two waiters came in carrying a table; a third followed with a cloth and silver. When the table was set one of the waiters said:

"Mr. Willoughby wants to know if he can come back now."

"Sure," said Olga, "tell him to come right back."

"Shall we start to serve?"

"Yeah," said Olga, "right away."

When the waiters had gone, Joe said:

"I'm getting fed up with this Willoughby guy. He's a dumb egg."

"Sure he's dumb," said Olga, "but I don't hold that against him. What I like about the bird is that he don't get his hand stuck in his pocket when the boy comes around with the bill."

"He sure don't, that's a fact," said Joe, laughing.

"Well, then don't be so particular," said Olga; "guys like him are few and far between."

Willoughby tapped lightly on the door and then came in. He was freshly shaven and he looked chubby and boyish.

Joe got up and shook hands with him. Olga said:

"Was you out front?"

"Yes," said Willoughby; "by the way, Joe, what was all the commotion?"

"See," said Joe, turning to Olga. "She thought I was making it up, Mr. Willoughby."

"No, he wasn't making it up," said Willoughby, serious. "I never heard such a scream in my life."

"Don't remind me," said Joe; "boy, my hair stood straight up."

A waiter came in carrying a wine bucket, followed by another waiter carrying the soup.

"Well," said Willoughby, "shall we monjay, as they say in France?"

"Oui, monsieur," said Olga.

"Sure," said Joe, "I'm ready for the feed-bag in any language."

They sat down. One of the waiters poured the wine. Willoughby held his glass up to the light.

"I hope you like this stuff," he said, "it's out of my own cellar."

"I'd like to sleep in that cellar," said Olga.

"Well," said Willoughby, "you have a standing invitation."

They ate in silence for a moment, then Joe said :

"Say, Mr. Willoughby, what you suppose was the matter with that dame?"

"I couldn't say."

"Oh, forget it, Joe," said Olga, "she was probably full of hop."

3

WILLOUGHBY passed the cigarettes and they all left the table. Joe went back to the lounge, Olga sat in one of the armchairs, and Willoughby pulled up an ottoman and sat facing her.

Willoughby hesitated before he said :

"Olga, when we going to take that little trip?"

"I don't know," said Olga.

"What little trip?" asked Joe, looking at Olga.

"Why, I got a cabin up in Wisconsin," said Willoughby, "and I thought before it got cold it would be nice for Olga to go up and take a rest."

"Yeah?" said Joe.

As soon as Willoughby lowered his eyes, Olga winked at Joe.

"Maybe I could pull it," said Olga.

"Sure," said Joe, "Olga works too hard, that's a fact. A little rest wouldn't hurt her none."

"That's just what I was thinking," said Willoughby. "She could sure get a rest up there. I got a couple of nice motor boats and the fishing's great."

"Fishing!" said Olga, looking at Joe.

"Well," Willoughby considered, "maybe you wouldn't care for that, but there are a number of things you could do. Anyway, the air's great, nothing like this Chicago muck."

"Sounds good," said Olga.

The waiters came to take away the table, but they were immediately followed by DeVoss, who motioned them out. There was something so strange about DeVoss's actions that Joe sat up and stared at him. DeVoss said:

"Joe, there's a couple of guys looking for you."

"Yeah?" said Joe. "What kind of guys?"

"Bulls," said DeVoss, "what you been up to?"

Olga got to her feet and stood staring at DeVoss. Willoughby exclaimed:

"What's all this! What's all this!"

Joe took an automatic from his hip pocket and put it in Olga's dressing-table. Olga took hold of DeVoss's arm and said:

"Tell them Joe ain't here. Joe, honey, beat it. I'll see if I can find out what it's all about."

Willoughby was staring stupefied at Joe. He pointed to the dressing-table.

"What do you carry that thing for?" he demanded.

Olga said:

"Oh, be quiet!"

Joe grinned at Willoughby.

"Just in case," he said.

"Listen, Olga," said DeVoss, "this is serious. I could tell the way they acted. I told them I didn't think Joe was here but they just laughed."

Joe stood undecided.

"Joe," DeVoss went on, "remember that time Mr. Rico was over here and a couple of bulls shadowed him? Well, the big one's here."

"Flaherty!" cried Joe.

Olga gave Joe a push.

"Beat it, Joe. You know them bulls. They'll frame you."

"O.K., honey," said Joe.

"Why, Joe," said Willoughby, "you mean to tell me you're in some kind of trouble?"

"Oh, be quiet," said Olga.

Joe grabbed his hat from a chair and started for the door.

"Goodbye, honey," he said to Olga, "you'll hear from me."

"Better face the music," said Willoughby.

"Go out through the kitchen," said DeVoss.

Joe opened the door but closed it immediately and said.

"It's all up. Here they come."

He looked in agony at Olga. Wasn't this just his goddamn luck! Penned up in a room three stories above the pavement. He made a dash for the dressing-table, but Olga grabbed his arm.

"For God's sake, Joe," said DeVoss, "don't cause no trouble in my place. I don't know what they want you for and I don't give a damn. I'll get you a lawyer and see you through, but, for God's sake, don't do no shooting in my place."

Willoughby, stunned, sat staring till his cigarette burned his fingers, then he said:

"Don't worry, Joe. I'll see you through too."

"Goddamn it," cried Joe, "you think I'm gonna let 'em take me like I was a purse-snatcher on his first stand."

He pushed Olga away from him and was pulling at the dressing-table drawer when the door opened and Flaherty came in, followed by Spike Rieger. Flaherty had his right hand in his coat pocket.

"Joe," said Flaherty, "step away from that drawer and make it snappy."

Joe knew Flaherty's reputation. That boy used his rod and argued afterwards. Joe moved away from the dressing-table and stood staring at the floor.

"What's the idea, Flaherty?" he demanded.

"Well," said Flaherty, "we've got a big audience here and I

ain't much on embarrassing people, so you better just come along and we'll have a nice little talk."

"Aw, can that," said Joe.

Willoughby walked over to Flaherty.

"My name's Willoughby," he said, "John C. Willoughby. I suppose you've heard of me. Say, what's this all about anyway? Why, I've known Joe for nearly a year and as far as I know he's a nice young fellow."

"Yeah," said Flaherty, "Joe's a pretty smooth young fellow, but we caught up with him."

"Well," said Willoughby, "I don't know what he's done, but I'm willing to go on his bail."

Flaherty turned to Rieger.

"I don't suppose there'll be much talk about bail, do you, Spike?"

Rieger grinned and shook his head.

"No bail!" Willoughby exclaimed.

"Aw, it's just one of their wise frame-ups, Mr. Willoughby," said Joe, but his face was white.

"Well, we'll see about this," said Willoughby. "I'll have my lawyer down in half an hour."

"Listen," said Flaherty, "there ain't nobody gonna see this bird for twenty-four hours."

Olga flung herself on the lounge and began to cry.

"And let me give you an earful, Mr. Willoughby," said Flaherty; "for a guy of your class you sure ain't very careful about who you mix up with. These two birds here are taking you, see, and if I was you I'd snap out of it and forget all about getting a lawyer."

"If that ain't a bull for you," said Joe.

"Don't pay any attention to him, Jack," said Olga.

"Certainly not," said Willoughby.

"All right, Spike," said Flaherty, "I guess we wasted enough time on these birds. Put the cuffs on him."

Olga jumped up and made a grab for Rieger, but DeVoss caught her from the back and held her.

"You can't do nothing that way, Olga," he said, "you'll just make it tough for Joe."

Olga screamed with rage and kicked back at DeVoss.

"Ain't dames awful?" said Flaherty.

Willoughby went over to Olga and tried to talk to her, but she continued to struggle. Rieger took out his handcuffs and walked over to Joe.

"Wait a minute," said Joe, "you can't put no bracelets on me. Where's your warrant?"

Rieger took the warrant out of his pocket and handed it to Joe. Joe read it slowly, then, without comment, handed it back.

"Well, Joe," said Flaherty.

Joe didn't say anything; he just held out his wrists.

"What do they want you for, Joe?" cried Olga.

"Never mind," said Joe, "they ain't got no case."

Olga stopped struggling.

"You mean it, Joe?"

"Sure," said Joe, "they ain't got no case at all. I'll be out in twenty-four hours."

"Shall I get my lawyer?" asked Willoughby.

"Ain't much use," said Joe.

DeVoss came over to Flaherty and said:

"Listen, Mr. Flaherty, take him out through the kitchen, can't you? I can't have cops coming in here pinching people."

"You got a nerve," said Flaherty; "why, I ought to pull you in for complicity. Didn't you come back here and tip Joe off?"

DeVoss got pale.

"Honest to God, I didn't tip him off. I just told him a couple of guys wanted to see him."

"Pipe down," said Flaherty. "Come on, Joe, let's take a ride."

Joe's face was ghastly, but he grinned.

"O.K.," he said; "it's the first ride I ever took with any of you birds."

"Well, I hope it's the last," said Flaherty.

"Want me to come down and see you, Joe?" asked Olga.

"No," said Joe.

They put Joe between two policemen in the back seat of the police car. Rieger and Flaherty sat in front. The traffic was light as it was nearly three o'clock in the morning. Rieger drove carelessly, one hand on the wheel most of the time, and talked to Flaherty.

"Boy," said Joe, "that bird don't care how he drives."

"You ain't got far to go," said one of the policemen.

"No, but I ain't sure of getting there."

The policemen laughed.

"Say," said Joe, "can I smoke?"

One of the policemen leaned forward.

"Say, chief, can this bird smoke?"

"No," said Flaherty; "what the hell you think this is, Joe! Maybe we better pick up a couple of girls for you."

The policemen laughed.

"Funny thing," said Joe, "you know, Flaherty, a friend of mine told me the other day that he didn't think you'd live long."

"Yeah," said Flaherty, "I know that friend of yours. He ain't looking any too healthy himself."

For as late as it was there was a good deal of activity at the station. A dozen plain-clothes men were waiting in the big room, when they brought Joe in, and the Assistant County Prosecutor was standing at the desk talking to the sergeant.

"Looks like big doings," said Joe.

"Shut up," said Flaherty; "recess is over. You open your mouth again and I'll close it for you."

They took Joe up to the desk to book him.

"Well, you got him," said the prosecutor, looking Joe over.

"Yeah, we got him," said Flaherty. "Did you chase the newspaper guys?"

"Yeah," said the prosecutor, "there won't be any leaks to this."

"O.K.," said Flaherty.

The sergeant nodded to him.

"All right, chief."

Flaherty took Joe by the arm.

"All right, Joe," he said, "we're gonna give you a nice little room."

"With bath?" asked Joe.

"Listen, boy," said Flaherty, "we're gonna take all that smartness out of you."

Joe didn't say anything. He was trying to keep up his front until they locked him in the cell, but he was ready to drop. They had him; they sure to God had him.

The turnkey swung the big barrel door wide. Flaherty took Joe to the door of his cell, unlocked the handcuffs, and gave him a push.

"All right, boy," he said, "I'll be back later."

"Listen, Flaherty," said Joe, "can't I even have a smoke?"

Flaherty laughed, motioned for the turnkey to lock the cell door, and disappeared down the corridor.

"Say, buddy," said Joe to the turnkey, "can't you get me a pack of cigarettes?"

"Nothing doing," said the turnkey, "not for fifty bucks. I got strict orders on you, boy."

The turnkey went away. Joe stood in the middle of his cell for a moment, then he climbed up on his bunk and looked out the window. Far away down a side street he saw a big electric sign : DANCING.

Joe flung himself down on his bunk. They had him; they sure to God did.

"If I can only stick it out!" he said.

4

Joe awoke from a doze and turned to look out the window. Still dark. He couldn't have been asleep long. Wasn't it never going to get light! He got up and walked to the front of his cell. It wouldn't be so bad if there were some other guys to talk to; but the cells on either side of him were vacant; also the ones across the corridor.

"They sure ain't taking no chances with me," said Joe.

He began to feel very uneasy. Something seemed to be dragging at his stomach and he had a rotten taste in his mouth.

"Some of that highhat grub I et," said Joe.

The turnkey came down the corridor and stopped in front of Joe's cell.

"Say, buddy," he said, "they'll be wanting you up front pretty soon."

"Yeah?" said Joe. "Listen, can't you do me a favour and get me a pack of cigs. I got plenty of money. Ask the sergeant."

"Can't cut it," said the turnkey.

"What's doing up front?" asked Joe.

"A show-up."

"Yeah?" said Joe; then, "listen, I'll give you a couple of bucks for some cigs."

The turnkey laughed.

"Say, there's a guy in 18 that'd give me a hundred berries for some snow. Not a chance. They sure are putting the clamps on us now. It's that goddamn Crime Commission business. Tough on you birds."

"Ain't it!" said Joe.

The turnkey went away. Joe threw himself down on his bunk. Yeah, now it was coming. That goddamn peroxide dame had sure put the skids under him. Well, there you was! Can't tell how things are going to break. If he'd've been wise he'd've sent Olga to see the Big Boy or Rico. But then there's no use letting a dame get too familiar with everything. Anyway, he had an alibi. But Flaherty was a rough agent and you could never tell what he would pull. Joe felt mechanically for his absent cigarette case.

"Hell," he said, "I lost my head! I lost my head! Rico ought to put a hunk of lead in me. As long as I been in the game and then don't know no better. God, but I was dumb."

He turned over irritably and sat up. He heard the keys clanking down the corridor. A policeman stopped in front of his door and called:

"All right, dago."

Joe got up. The turnkey unlocked the door. There were two policemen and a plain-clothes man standing a little way down the corridor. When Joe came out one of the policemen said:

"There's the guy that plugged Courtney."

They stared at him. Joe felt sick at his stomach.

"Yeah," said the plain-clothes man, "they won't do much to that bird."

The turnkey took Joe by the arm.

"All right, kid," he said.

Joe walked between the turnkey and the policeman, who had called him. They took him into a big room where there were three policemen and about a dozen prisoners. Joe saw Bugs Liska, Steve Gollancz's lieutenant. They exchanged a glance.

A police sergeant got to his feet and shouted:

"All right, you birds, let's go."

The turnkey pushed Joe into line. A big door was swung open and he saw a small, brilliantly lighted room with a crowd of people lining the walls. Joe looked for the peroxide blonde. There she was, pale and hardboiled, between two bulls. Joe startled. God, he had her now. She was standing side of Courtney when he dropped. Joe began to sweat.

The line in single file was herded in. Bugs Liska, who was in front of Joe, whispered:

"Say, what's this all about?"

The sergeant heard him and leaping across the room grabbed him by the shoulder.

"Any more of that," said the sergeant, "and some of you bad eggs is gonna get cracked."

"Drop dead," said Liska.

Joe found himself face to face with the blonde. She stared at him. Flaherty walked along the line and examined the prisoners. When he got to Joe, Joe looked away.

"How's that bath?" asked Flaherty.

"O.K.," said Joe.

Liska said:

"Say, Irish, what's this all about?"

"Shut your dirty mouth," said Flaherty.

A man Joe had never seen before, a big husky man with curly grey hair, went over to the blonde and said:

"Is he in that bunch, Mrs. Weil?"

The blonde nodded.

"Well, Mrs. Weil, this is a very serious matter so don't make any mistakes. Now if you're sure he's in that bunch, point him out."

The blonde compressed her lips and walked over to Joe.

"There he is. There's the dirty skunk."

"Jesus," said Liska, glancing at Joe, "it's your funeral, hunh?"

The blonde stood glaring at Joe.

"I hope they hang you," she cried, "shooting a guy like Jim Courtney."

"I never shot him," said Joe.

"Shut up," said Flaherty. "All right, sergeant, march 'em out."

In the big room Liska said:

"Joe, it sure looks tough for you."

"They can't prove nothing," said Joe.

The sergeant rushed at them.

"Where do you birds think you're at!" he cried.

Stepping back, he struck Joe a hard blow with his fist. Mechanically Joe set himself and raised his hands, then, coming to himself, he dropped his hands and stood looking at the floor. Liska said:

"Say, sergeant, I guess I can go home, can't I? My old mother'll be worried to death."

The sergeant stared at Liska, then he laughed.

"I'm gonna hang on to you just for fun," he said.

"Yeah?" said Liska. "Well not long, cause Steve's gonna spring me."

The sergeant motioned for the turnkey.

"Lock the dago up," he said; "you plant yourself over there in a chair, Bugs."

Joe lay down and tried to sleep. Over his head the barred window began to get grey. Morning sure was slow in coming.

Of a sudden he thought of Red Gus. He got to his feet and began to walk back and forth. Yeah, they sure put the rope on old Gus and there wasn't a tougher guy in the world. Yeah, he was so tough he didn't die right away and kept kicking. Cops fainted and all that stuff. Joe climbed up on his bunk and stood tiptoe to look out the window. Morning was coming. He saw the milk wagon passing the jail. How come he had to think of Red Gus?

He thought he heard a noise and turned around. There

were two cops standing in front of his cell, looking at him. Joe felt uneasy.

"Want me?" he called.

They didn't say anything; they just stood there looking, then went away.

Joe got down from the window and sat on his bunk. No use trying to sleep. Down the corridor someone began to scream. The turnkey passed his cell on the run. Joe felt his hair stirring and sweat stood out on his forehead.

"Christ," he said, "it's only that dope."

In a minute the turnkey came back and stopped at Joe's door.

"Couple of guys coming back to take a look at you," he said.

"Yeah?" said Joe; "say, what was all the noise?"

"The dope blew his top again," said the turnkey; "the Doc's gonna give him a shot pretty soon."

The big man with the curly grey hair, Flaherty, and two policemen came down the corridor.

"All right," said Flaherty, "let him out."

The turnkey unlocked the door and pushed Joe into the corridor. They all stood staring at Joe; nobody said anything.

Finally the grey-haired man said:

"Well, it's too bad. Nice-looking boy."

"Yeah," said Flaherty, "but he's hell with a gun."

Joe didn't say anything. But Flaherty said:

"Joe, I never thought you was the kind of bird that'd shoot a guy in the back."

Joe didn't say anything.

"Hanging's too good for you, Joe."

"Poor old Jim never even had a gun on him. You lousy dago!" cried one of the policemen, and took a step toward Joe.

Flaherty motioned him back.

"Just let the law take its course, Luke," he said, "they'll hang this baby sure."

"Will they?" said Joe.

The grey-haired man shook his finger at Joe.

"Yes, my boy, I'm afraid they will."

"They can't prove nothing on me," said Joe; "I wasn't even

in that end of town the night Courtney was bumped off. That dame's full of hop."

One of the policemen stepped past Flaherty and knocked Joe down. Flaherty grabbed the policeman and pushed him back. Joe got to his feet and stood holding his jaw.

"I'm gonna put it to you birds for this," said Joe.

Both of the policemen made a rush at Joe, but Flaherty held them back.

"Well," said Flaherty, "got an eyeful, Mr. McClure?"

Joe stared at the grey-haired man. So this was the Crime Commission guy that was kicking up all the row. Joe took a good look at him so he'd know him the next time he saw him. Maybe, if things broke right, he could deliver a nice package at the bird's house some morning.

"Yes," said Mr. McClure, "lock him up, turnkey."

The turnkey took Joe by the arm and flung him into his cell. Joe fell on his hands and knees.

"Say," said Joe, "what's the idea?"

The turnkey came over and put his face against the bars.

"Orders, buddy," he said, then he went away.

Yeah, it was orders all right. They wasn't going to let up on him till he spilled something. Joe felt panicky. He flung himself face down on his bunk and began to sob.

"Won't I never get out of here?" he said.

They had been questioning Joe for over two hours. He sat under a blazing light and they sat round him in the darkness. Joe was so thirsty that he could hardly swallow. They took turns at him: first, Mr. McClure, then Flaherty, then Rieger. Flaherty sat near him and when he was slow with his answers rapped him over the knuckles with a ruler. But Joe stuck it out.

The turnkey took him back to his cell and gave him some water. Joe took a big drink, then lay down on his bunk and tried to sleep, but it was no use. He felt hot all over and his tongue was swollen.

He put his hands under his head and lay looking at the square spots of sunshine in the dark corridor.

"God," he said, "I can't stand much of this."

In five minutes the turnkey came back.

"They want you again, kid," he said.

"God, I can't move," said Joe.

The turnkey unlocked the door and came into the cell.

"Get on your feet," he said, "and snap it up. The prosecutor's in there now and you're gonna ketch hell."

Joe got slowly to his feet and the turnkey led him down the corridor.

5

SAM VETTORI sat half-dozing in an armchair watching a crap game. It was about eleven o'clock in the morning and most of the blinds were still down. All the wheels were covered and the chairs were piled up on the tables. The game was desultory as nobody had much money. As it wasn't a house game, but merely some of the Vettori gang amusing themselves, Sam occasionally staked one or another of the players.

Since the rise of Rico, Sam had confined his efforts to the managing of Little Arnie's old joint. He was making money hand over fist and he was content to sit all day in his armchair and superintend the work of his employees. He drank wine by the gallon and ate plate after plate of spaghetti. In a month he put on fifteen pounds. As he was fat to begin with, this added poundage made him immense. His aquiline features were puffed out nearly beyond recognition and there were rolls of fat at the base of his skull. Sam had loosed the reins and gone slack. Formerly, effort had kept him in better condition, but now, perfectly at ease, free of responsibility, the deadly lethargy which had threatened him all his life took possession of him.

Sam crossed his legs with difficulty and took out a stogie. The crap game had ended in an argument. Kid Bean loudly contended that he had been gypped.

"Shut up, you guys," said Sam, "I'm doing you a favour to let you shoot in here. Any more of this kind of stuff and you don't do it no more. If you guys'd save your money you wouldn't have to be fighting over two bits."

"Aw, rest your jaw," said Kid Bean.

Joe Peeper took the dice and flung them out the window.
"Them babies'll never bother me no more," said Joe.
"Can you beat that!" said Kid Bean.
"Well," said Sam, "since Blackie's got all the jack, the rest of you guys can pitch pennies. Listen, Kid, don't forget you owe me two bucks."
"You can take it out of my hide," said the Kid.
"Your hide ain't worth it," said Sam.
Chesty, the doorman, came out of Sam's office rubbing his eyes.
"Sam," he said, "Scabby wants to see you."
"Tell him to come out here," said Sam.
"No," said Chesty, "he wants to see you private."
"Hey, Sam," said Kid Bean, "give us a deck of cards, will you?"
"No," said Sam, "you don't even know what they're for." He pulled himself slowly to his feet and turning to Chesty went on: "Get these guys a pack of cards and lock 'em up some place. They'd bump each other off for two bits and I don't want this nice carpet spoiled."
Yawning and stretching, Sam went into his office and shut the door. Scabby was standing in the middle of the room, biting his nails.
"Want a bottle of wine or something, Scabby?" asked Sam.
"Christ, no!" cried Scabby.
Sam stared at him, then dropped into a chair.
"Well," he said, "you look like you got something on your mind, so spill it."
Scabby was so nervous that he couldn't control the muscles of his face.
"You're goddamn right I got something on my mind," said Scabby, "Joe spilled the works."
Sam opened his eyes wide.
"Joe who?"
"Joe Massara," said Scabby, "they nabbed him on the Courtney business and he squawked."
Sam's jaw fell and he ran his hands over his face in a bewildered way.
"Yeah?" he said.
"It's the God's truth," said Scabby; "boy, the bulls sure

played this one slick. Listen, I didn't even know nothing about it. They kept the newspaper guys out and when a couple guys who were in the know came looking for Joe they told them that they must have him at the Chicago Avenue station. And out at Chicago Avenue they sent 'em some place else. Yeah, it's all over now."

This was too much for Sam. He just sat there staring at Scabby.

"God, Sam," said Scabby, astonished, "don't you get me? It's all over. Listen, if it wasn't for you I'd be on my way right now. I don't know whether I'll be named or not, but I ain't taking no chances. Love of God, Sam, don't just sit there. You got to do something."

"Joe spilled everything?" asked Sam, taking it in slowly.

"Yeah, he stuck it out for four hours, but he didn't have a chance."

There was a flash of the old Sam Vettori. He got up and took Scabby by the arm.

"Is Rico wised up?"

"No," said Scabby.

"All right," said Sam, "you keep your mouth shut."

"You don't have to tell me," said Scabby.

Sam looked about him, bewildered.

"But, good God," he cried, "what am I gonna do?"

"Well," said Scabby, "I got a can down here and I'm hitting East. Want to go with me? I'll take a chance."

Sam looked his bewilderment. Things were moving too fast for him. Why, he hadn't been out of Chicago for twenty years. He hadn't been out of Little Italy for over five. Just pick up and beat it.

"What the hell!" said Sam, "I got a good business. . . . God, what am I gonna do?"

Scabby stared at him.

"Why, Sam," he said, "you must be losing your mind."

Sam wiped the sweat from his face and sank back into his chair.

"Joe spilled it, hunh? Rico said he'd turn yellow."

Scabby took him under the arms and tried to pull him to his feet, but Sam pushed him away.

"No use running," he said, "they'll get you sure. I ain't gonna go running all over hell and back and a bunch of bulls chasing me."

Scabby swore violently in Italian.

"No," said Sam, "no use running."

"Well," said Scabby, "this bird's gonna pull his freight. Sam, you must be full of hop."

Sam sat staring at his shoes.

"Listen," said Scabby, "I can't waste no more time. Are you gonna pull out or ain't you?"

Sam didn't say anything.

"O.K.," said Scabby; "I'm moving."

"Wait," cried Sam. "Scabby, listen to me. I been good to you, ain't I?"

"You sure have."

"I give you the money to bring your old man over here, didn't I? And I give you the money to bury him, didn't I?"

"You sure did."

"Well, listen, Scabby, if Rico gets away, pop him. God-damn him; he's busted us all. Pop him, Scabby, for old Sam."

"He won't get away," said Scabby.

"You don't know that guy," said Sam, getting shakily to his feet; "sure to God as I'm a Catholic, you don't know that guy. He's got a run of luck and it may last."

"If he gets away I'll pop him," said Scabby.

The door was flung violently open and Killer Pepi stepped in.

"I heard you bastards," he said. "The Kid told me there was something up. Double-crossing the boss, hunh?"

"Go to hell," said Sam.

Scabby raised his gun but it misfired. The Killer shot from his hip, then ran out, slamming the door.

"Did he plug you, Scabby?" cried Sam.

"No," said Scabby, "but I heard her sing."

The window behind Scabby had a bullet hole in it.

"He'll spill it sure," said Sam, his face puckered.

"Won't do him no good," said Scabby, " 'cause the bulls are on their way. Well, Sam, I'm moving."

Sam just looked at him. Scabby raised the window and climbed out on the fire-escape.

"Love of God, Sam," said Scabby, "you got to do something."

Sam took his hat from the hook.

"I'll go see the Big Boy."

"It won't do you no good, Sam."

They heard someone running down the hall, then, there was a shot, followed by a rush of feet. Chesty flung open the door.

"The bulls!" he cried.

Scabby disappeared down the fire-escape. Sam took out his automatic and put his back against the wall. Spike Rieger put his head in the door, then drew it back hastily.

"Sam," he called, "better give up."

"All right," said Sam, flinging his gun on the floor.

Spike Rieger came in followed by two policemen.

"Put the cuffs on him," said Spike.

Sam held out his hands and one of the policemen snapped on the handcuffs.

"Spike," said Sam, "did you pick the Killer up on the way in?"

"No," said Spike, "we don't want him for nothing." Turning to the policemen Spike said: "All right, put him in the wagon."

"Listen, Spike," said Sam, "did you get Rico?"

"I don't know," said Spike. "Flaherty's after him. I guess you know Gentleman Joe squawked, don't you?"

"Yeah," said Sam, indifferently, "but you ain't got no case against me."

Spike laughed.

6

The killer knocked at Rico's door but got no response. He knocked again and again, then, getting impatient, he put his shoulder to the door and flung it open. No Rico. The Killer stood in the hall, wondering where Rico could have gone. From the landing above him, the landlady yelled:

"Hey, what did you do to that door?"

"The hell with the door," said Pepi; "do you know where the guy that lives there is?"

"No," said the landlady, "but I seen him go out with a fellow."

"A little fellow."

Otero! Killer took the stairs at a jump but slowed his pace as he reached the main floor. There was a police car at the kerb. Flaherty got out leisurely and stood talking to one of the policemen in the front seat. Pepi went over to him.

"Looking for the boss?"

"Yeah," said Flaherty, "the Big Boy sent me down. I want to have a talk with him."

"Yeah?" said Pepi. "Getting wise to yourself, hunh?"

"Rico was always O.K. with me."

"That's the talk," said Pepi. "Well, the boss is upstairs by himself."

When Flaherty and one of his men had gone into the building, the Killer grinned at the others and walked slowly away, but, as soon as he had turned the corner, he broke into a run.

There were two little Italian kids sitting on the steps of the stairway that led up to Otero's. They made way for Pepi.

"Otero upstairs?" he asked.

One of the kids said:

"That funny little guy?"

"Yeah," said Pepi.

"I think I seen him go up."

"Yeah," said the other kid, "I seen him."

Pepi took the stairs at a run and rapped at Otero's door. Seal Skin opened it a few inches but Pepi pushed her aside and walked in. Otero was sitting with his feet on the bed, smoking a big cigar.

"Where's the boss?" asked Pepi.

"At Blondy's. What's the matter?"

"Joe squawked," said Pepi, "and the bulls is looking for Rico. Get your coat on and beat it, Otero. I'll go after the boss."

"Bulls looking for me too?"

"Sure," said Pepi, "it's the Courtney business. You beat it, Otero. This ain't no picnic."

"No," said Otero, "I go with Rico."

"You damn dummy," said Seal Skin.

"Yeah," said Pepi, "you beat it, Otero. Get out of town. They don't want me for nothing. I'll see if I can't get Rico on the phone; if I can't I'll go after him. Listen, the bulls is over at Rico's right now."

"Caramba!" cried Otero, and, slipping his automatic into his coat pocket, he ran out into the hall and down the stairs.

"The damn dummy!" said Seal Skin.

Pepi stood looking at Seal Skin, then he said:

"Sure he's a damn dummy, but he's right."

Before Otero had gone half a block in the direction of Blondy's, he saw a police car coming towards him. He ducked into a drugstore. It was empty except for a clerk who stood staring at Otero.

"Show me the back way out, you!" said Otero.

"Say!" said the clerk.

Otero took out his gun. The clerk threw himself down behind the counter. Otero ran out through the prescription room and found the back door, which opened into an alley. One end of the alley was blind, the other came out onto a busy street. Otero ran toward the open end, praying in Spanish.

All along the kerbs on both sides of the street pushcarts were drawn up and peddlers were calling their wares. A slow-moving crowd of Little Italians blocked the pavements. Otero, because of his size, disappeared into the crowd, and, although he was forced to go slowly, he was safe from observation. Half a block from Blondy's he ducked down an alley, crossed a long cement court and climbed the fire-escape.

Blondy's bedroom window was locked. Otero beat on it with his fist. For a moment there was no response, then he saw the bedroom door open slowly and Blondy's face appeared. She ran over and unlocked the window, then she turned and called:

"Rico, it's The Greek."

Rico came into the bedroom. He had his hat on.

"Did Pepi get you?"

"No, what the hell?"

The phone rang and Blondy went to answer it. "They got Joe and he squawked," said Otero. Rico looked at him.

Blondy came running back. "My God, Rico," she said, "the bulls're after you. Joe squealed. You ought to plugged that softie, Rico. You ought to plugged him."

Rico stood in the middle of the room, staring. By an effort of the will, he rid himself of an attitude of mind which had been growing on him since his interviews with Montana and the Big Boy. He was nobody, nobody. Worse than nobody. The bulls wanted him now and they wanted him bad. Goodbye dollar cigars and crockery at one grand, goodbye swell food and tuxedos and security. Rico was nobody. Just a lonely Youngstown yegg that the bulls wanted. His face was ghastly.

He swung his fist at the air.

"I ought to plugged him! I ought to plugged him!"

Otero stood staring at Rico. Blondy was putting on her hat.

"All right," said Rico, "let's go."

Blondy said:

"Take me, Rico."

Rico shook his head.

"Nothing doing, Blondy. I'm travelling fast and I can't be bothered with no dame."

"Jesus, Rico," said Blondy, unable to realize what had happened, "everything was going so nice."

"Sure," said Rico, "but it's all over now and that's that. You stay planted, Blondy, and as soon as I get a chance I'll send you a stake."

Otero crawled out the window onto the fire-escape and Rico followed him. Blondy began to scream.

"Shut your mouth," said Rico, "and if the bulls come up the front way kid 'em along. Make 'em think you got me hid, see?"

"O.K., Rico," said Blondy.

Otero and Rico went down the fire-escape. They stopped at the foot of the fire-escape and Rico took Otero by the arm.

"Listen," he said, "here's the dope. We got to get to Ma Magdalena's. She's got most of my jack and a good hide-out. It ain't gonna be easy, because the bulls're probably scattered all around. But once we get there, we're O.K."

"All right," said Otero.

They started. Rico knew every alley in the district, and he led Otero by such a safe route that they were soon within a block and a half of Ma Magdalena's without having crossed a main thoroughfare.

"Now," said Rico, "we got to watch our step. If the bulls are cruising, they're cruising this street sure."

"All right," said Otero.

"Listen," said Rico, "don't be afraid to use your gat if the fun begins. They can only hang you once."

"I ain't afraid," said Otero.

They left the alley and were half way across the street when somebody shouted at them to halt. Without turning, they broke into a run.

"It's only one bull," said Rico.

A bullet sang over them and they heard the blast of a policeman's whistle. Otero stopped in his tracks, turned, took a steady aim and fired. The policeman staggered forward three or four steps and fell to his knees.

"Got him," said Otero.

Rico turned. The policeman was kneeling in the middle of the street, trying to steady his hand for a shot.

"Duck," cried Rico, simultaneously with the firing of the policeman's gun.

Otero twisted sideways, looked at Rico with surprise, then dropped his gun, and began to walk up the alley, holding his stomach. Rico put his arm around him and, pulling him over to the side of the alley where he could keep a telephone pole between them and the policeman, guided him along. But after a few steps, Otero pulled away from Rico and cried:

"Run, Rico, run. They got me sure. I can't feel nothing."

Rico grabbed him and tried to pull him along, but he resisted.

"Goddamn you, Rico," cried Otero, "run! I can't go no farther. I'm done for."

Rico heard the roar of a police car. He released Otero, who staggered away from him and then fell flat on his back.

"Run, Rico," said Otero.

Rico climbed a fence, ran up through a filthy back yard, and in an open back door. There was a young Italian girl sweeping in the hall. At Rico's sudden appearance, she dropped her broom and flattened herself against the wall. Rico took her by the arm.

"Listen, sister," he said, "the bulls're after me. I'm going out the front way, see, but if the bulls come through here you tell 'em I hopped the fence next door and doubled back. Got it?"

"Yes sir," said the girl, then looking up at Rico, "I know you."

"Yeah?" said Rico. "Well, do your stuff then, sister."

In the alley behind the house there was a shriek of brakes and someone cried in a loud voice:

"He went in that way!"

The girl picked up her broom and went on sweeping. Rico ran out through the front hall, down the long flight of stone steps, and crossed the street leisurely.

7

MA MAGDALENA let him in at the alley door.

"Well, Rico," she said; "got yourself in a nice fix, didn't you?"

Rico grinned.

"Yeah," he said, "who told you?"

"The bulls were here and searched the place."

"Didn't find the hide-out, did they?"

Ma Magdalena laughed.

"What a chance!"

Rico followed Ma down into the basement. She led him through a short tunnel and back into the hide-out. A small, round opening just large enough to admit one person had been pierced in a heavy stone wall. In front of the wall rows of pine shelves had been built and these were filled with canned goods. The section of the shelves which hid the opening was hinged and could be swung open.

Rico followed Ma through the opening and came out into a little room with a cot in one corner, a table, and one chair. Rico took off his hat and sat down.

"They got The Greek," he said.

"Yeah?" said Ma.

Rico took out a cigar and lit it.

"Listen," he said, "I want to stay here a couple of days. Then I'm gonna pull out. Get me some magazines and keep me posted."

"All right," said Ma, "but it's gonna cost you, because I'm taking chances, see, I'm taking big chances."

"Well," said Rico, "you got my roll, help yourself."

Ma Magdalena smiled broadly.

"That's the talk, Rico. Old Ma'll sure take care of you."

"O.K.," said Rico; "now, get this: in two days I want a car."

"Arrigo's got a car. If we go hooking one, it might spoil your get-away."

"That's good," said Rico; "all right, I want a jumper suit, you know, one of them suits like a garage mechanic wears, and a razor."

"All right," said Ma Magdalena.

When she had gone, Rico took off his coat and shoes, and lay down on the cot. His nerves were jumpy and he couldn't seem to get settled. He flung his cigar away and turned his face to the wall.

"Just when I thought things was on the up and up," he said.

Rico felt resentful, but his resentment was not directed at any specific group or person; it was vague as yet. He turned from side to side on his cot, then he gave it up.

Ma Magdalena came back with a big mug of coffee and a couple of papers. Rico sat down at the table.

"They got Sam," said Ma.

"Well," said Rico, "that's hips for Sam."

Rico took the papers from her and glanced at the headlines.

GENTLEMAN JOE WILTS
GANG CHIEF NAMED AS SLAYER

Ma Magdalena went out. Rico sat reading the paper and sipping his coffee.

Gentleman Joe Massara looks more like a movie actor

than a gunman. When arrested he was wearing an expensive tuxedo and the rings that were taken from him are valued at $3000.

"To hell with that," said Rico.

He read on:

Cesare Bandello, known as Rico, the Vettori gang chief, was named as the actual slayer of Courtney....

"Yeah," said Rico, "and I'm the only one they ain't gonna get."

PART 7

I

It was dark when Rico reached the outskirts of Hammond. He drove into a field, took the license plates off and buried them, and got out of his jumpers. Then he took some clean waste from the tool box and wiped the grease from his face.

"What a cinch," he said.

Things had gone a lot better than he had expected them to. There hadn't been a hitch of any kind. A motor cop out in Blue Island had waved to him even. Rico laughed. You never know. When you're looking for things to go right they never do. When you're looking for trouble, why, things are O.K. Yeah, funny!

Rico walked to the car line. He was wearing a plain, dark suit and an army shirt Arrigo had given him. He had shaved off his mustache and the hard, short bristles on his upper lip worried him. Rico felt very proud of his escape. It was a good idea to dress himself up like a garage mechanic and drive across town in broad daylight. Yeah, it was a good idea and if things broke right he'd write to one of the papers and tell them all about it. Only the postmark would give him away. Not so good. Well, anyway, he could tell Sansotta about it.

Rico got on a street-car.

"Well, how's things?" he said to the conductor.

"All right," said the conductor; "getting cooler, ain't it? Reckon we'll have winter before we know it."

"Yeah," said Rico.

2

Rico went up the alley at the side of Sansotta's place and knocked at the back door. It was a long time before somebody came and took a look at him through the shutter. A voice with a marked Italian accent said:

"Who are you?"

"Where's Sansotta?" asked Rico.

"What do you care?"

"Listen, buddy," said Rico, "don't get all het up. I'm right. Go tell Sansotta that Cesare wants him."

In a few minutes the door opened and a hand motioned for Rico to come in. The hall was dark and Rico stumbled going up the stairs. The look-out took hold of his arm.

"The boss's up in his room. I'll take you up. Where you from, buddy?"

"Youngstown," said Rico.

"Where's that?"

"Over east."

The look-out led Rico down a long, dark hallway and to a door at the end of it. Lights showed over a transom. The look-out knocked three times and the door was opened. Rico went in.

"Well," said Sansotta, locking the door, "here you are?"

"Yeah," said Rico.

Sansotta was a small, bowlegged Italian with a dark, scarred face. He had on a striped suit, brown and red, and a stiff collar the points of which were so high that his chin rested on them. There was a big diamond stud in his shirt-front.

"You must've got a break," said Sansotta.

Rico explained how he had got away.

"Pretty nifty," said Sansotta; "I got to hand it to you on that, Cesare."

"Yeah," said Rico, "it was a good idea."

Sansotta went over to a table, opened a drawer and took out a handbill which he gave to Rico. Rico smiled.

"Raised the ante, did they? Last I heard it was five grand."

Rico read the handbill over and over and stared at the Bertillon pictures.

"Them pictures don't look like me," he said.

Sansotta pursed his lips and scrutinized them.

"Not since you got the tickler off. No, and you look thinner in them pictures. How long ago was they taken?"

"About seven years ago."

The handbill read:

> Wanted for murder: Cesare Bandello, known as Rico, Age: 29. Height: 5 ft. 5 in. Weight: 125. Complexion: pale. Hair: black and wavy. Eyes: light, grey or blue. His face is thin and he walks with one foot slightly turned in. Does not take up with strangers. Solitary type, morose and dangerous. Reward $5000, offered by management of Casa Alvarado. $2000, offered by City of Chicago, for capture dead or alive.

"Well," said Sansotta, "where you headed for?"

"I'm gonna stick around here for a while," said Rico.

"Yeah?" said Sansotta; "pretty close to trouble, ain't it?".

"I don't know," said Rico, "they ain't got any idea which way I went. I got a big stake and I don't have to worry none."

"You sure went up fast over in the big burg," said Sansotta, looking at Rico with a sort of awe.

"Yeah," said Rico, "and the hell of it was, I was just getting started. Everything was on the up and up when one of the gang turned softie. Ain't that hell?"

Rico had been very much elated over his escape from Chicago, so elated in fact that he had forgotten all about his troubles; but, now that the excitement of the escape had passed, the thought of how much he had lost struck him full force. He felt resentful.

"Yeah," said Sansotta, "that's the way it goes. It's a tough game. They picked up two of my men last night."

"That so?" said Rico, paying no attention.

Sansotta got up.

"Well, Cesare," he said, "I got business or I'd stick around and chin with you. Want to stay here with me till things blow over?"

"Yeah," said Rico.

3

NIGHT after night Rico lay awake looking at the arc light outside his window. His mind was filled with resentment and he went over and over the incidents which had led to his fall. Now it was too late, he saw the mistakes he had made. He should have plugged Gentleman Joe; that's all. When a guy begins to turn softie, why there ain't no good in him. Yeah, he had been too easy. Another thing. He should have played Scabby up; that guy was in a position to do him all kinds of favours, but Scabby was a hard guy to get along with; he always thought somebody was trying to make a fool of him and he always had a chip on his shoulder.

Sometimes Rico would fall asleep for a little while, but his sleep was full of dreams and he would toss from side to side and wake up with a start. Then he would get up and smoke one cigarette after another and think about Montana and Little Arnie and the Big Boy. Often, in these short naps, he would see The Greek lying on his back in the alley, or the little Italian girl sweeping the hall, or Ma Magdalena helping him put the grease on his face. Then he would awake in confusion and stare at the unfamiliar arc light a long time before he could realize where he was.

In the day time it wasn't so bad. He could play cards with Sansotta and some of his gang, or shoot crap on a pool table in the back room. Rico always played to win and while the game was in progress he forgot his troubles. But even this was but a partial alleviation. He was nobody. Just an unknown wop who seemed to have unlimited resources. Sansotta was the only one who knew who he was. He had taken his uncle's name, Luigi De Angelo, and around Sansotta's he was called Youngstown Louis, or usually plain Louis. No, he was nobody. When a card game got hot and one of the players thought he was getting gypped, a look from Rico did not quiet the tumult as it had done in Little Italy. A look from Rico meant nothing. He was cursed with the rest of them. Often the desire to show these two-bit wops who they were yelling at would make him writhe in his chair, and his hand would move toward his armpit, but he couldn't risk it. He had his neck to think about, and there was Sansotta, a good guy, doing what he could for him. Rico kept saying to himself, you are nobody, nobody, but it was galling.

Sometimes he would go to his room early and just sit in the dark and think. He would imagine himself in the Big Boy's wonderful apartment; he would see the big pictures of the old time guys in their gold frames, the one grand crockery, and the library full of books; or he would recall the night when Little Arnie's Detroit toughs tried to bump him off and how when he came back to The Palermo the people stood on the chairs and shouted: "Rico! Rico!" God, it was hard to take!

The stories in the magazines about swell society people that he used to read with such eagerness failed to interest him now. After a paragraph or two he would fling the magazine aside and swear.

"Yeah," he would say, "ain't that great! The damn dressed-up softies. Got everything in the world and never had to turn a hand for it."

Rico was filled with resentment and when he spoke, rarely now, it was to denounce or ridicule something. The wops around Sansotta's, though they were obtuse enough, were not long in noticing this, and Rico began to be known as Crabby Louis.

They would say: "Well, Crabby Louis, it's your shot"; or "All right, Crabby, deal the cards."

The only thing that really interested Rico was the trial of Sam Vettori. Joe Massara, who had turned State's evidence, had been sentenced to life. "Lord," said Rico, when he read Joe's sentence, "I never thought they'd give Gentleman Joe a jolt like that after he turned State's. Them boys means business." Sam's trial had been rushed because of the hubbub raised by Mr. McClure and other influential men, and the outcome was never in doubt. Sam Vettori was sentenced to be hanged.

When Rico read the verdict he lay back in his chair and looked at the wall.

"Well, old Sam had a long whack at it," he said; "never seen the inside of a prison in his life. A guy's luck's bound to turn."

Then he went over in his mind the robbery of the Casa Alvarado and all the steps which had led to his own rise and fall.

"It made me and it broke me," he said.

On New Year's Eve Rico dressed up more than usual and went down into Sansotta's cabaret. It was jammed and unable to get a seat he went into Sansotta's office and had one of the waiters bring him a meal. He sat with the door open and watched the antics on the dance floor. There was plenty of liquor about and the crowd was pretty rough. Rico saw a big blonde dancing with a fat Italian. She gave him a look and he motioned for her to come in the office. She nodded. Rico got up and closed the door. In a few minutes the Blonde came in.

"Well, kid," she said, "what's on your mind?"

"I got a room upstairs," said Rico, "that ain't occupied."

"The hell you have," said the Blonde.

"Yeah," said Rico, "and I got a bank roll that ain't got any strings on it."

"Now you're talking," said the Blonde, putting her arm around Rico.

"Well," said Rico, "let's go."

"Listen," said the Blonde, "I'll be back after a while. I got a guy out here that's plenty tough and I got to humour him."

"Aw, hell," said Rico, "I'll take that toughness out of him. Stick around."

The Blonde looked at Rico and laughed.

"Say," she said, "you ain't big enough to talk so big."

"No," said Rico, resentful, "I ain't so big."
"Listen, honey," said the Blonde, "this boy would eat you alive."
"Yeah?" said Rico.
The fat Italian opened the door and came in.
"What's the idea, Mickey?" he said to the Blonde.
"Why, I just happened to bump into an old friend of mine," said the Blonde, scared.
Rico got up and stood looking at the fat Italian.
"What's it to you!" he said.
"Why, listen, kid," said the fat Italian, "you better go get your big brother cause if you make any more cracks I'm gonna dust off the furniture with you."
The Blonde took the fat Italian by the arm.
"Come on, Paul," she said, "let's go dance."
"Yeah," said Rico, "take that bird away before something happens to him."
The fat Italian pulled away from the Blonde and started towards Rico.
"That's one crack too many," he said.
But Rico, standing with his back against Sansotta's desk, perfectly calm, reached under his armpit and pulled his gun. The fat Italian hesitated and looked bewildered.
"Well," said Rico, "kind of lost your steam, didn't you?"
The fat Italian turned and looked at the Blonde.
"That's a nice boy friend you got," he said.
The Blonde stood there with her mouth open.
"All right, big boy," said Rico, "we can get along without you."
Sansotta opened the door and stood looking from one to the other.
"What's the matter, Paul?" he inquired.
The fat Italian pointed at Rico.
"That bird there tried to grab my girl, and when I told him about it he pulled a gat on me."
Sansotta's face darkened.
"Put that gun up, Louis," he said, staring hard at Rico; "where you think you're at? Listen, Paul, Louis's a new guy here and he don't know the ropes."
"Well," said the fat Italian, "he sure is quick with a gun."

"That's all right, Paul," said the Blonde, laughing, "he needs a handicap."

Rico, furious, put on his hat and started to go. But Sansotta said :

"Wait a minute, Louis, I want to see you." Then turning to the fat Italian: "I'm sure sorry this happened, but you know how it is when a guy don't know the ropes, he'll butt in where it ain't healthy to butt in, see? Louis's all right, but he's got a bad temper."

"Ain't he," said Paul. "Well, I guess we better be moving up town. I ain't any too anxious to hang around where you're liable to get bumped off."

"Aw, stick around, Paul," Sansotta implored; "you won't have no more trouble."

"No," said Paul, "I'll be moving. Come on, Mickey. I seen all of your boy friend that I want to see."

Sansotta followed them out into the cabaret, trying to persuade them to remain, but Paul went over to the check-window and got their wraps. Rico sat down and went on with his meal. Sansotta came in and slammed the door after him.

"Goddamn you, Cesare," he cried, "why don't you be more careful? That guy is Paolo, the political boss. He can close me up tomorrow if he wants too."

"Take it easy," said Rico; "how the hell did I know? You think I'm gonna let a guy take a bust at me?"

Sansotta took out a cigar and began to chew on it.

"Cesare," he said, "you got to be moving. I can't have you hanging around here no more. It's too dangerous."

Rico dropped his fork and stared at Sansotta.

"Giving me the go-by, hunh?"

"Yeah," said Sansotta, "you got to be moving."

Rico got to his feet and stood looking at Sansotta.

"Just on account of a small town ward-heeler," he said; "why that guy couldn't boss a section gang. You're a hell of a guy, Sansotta. After all the jack I spent in this dump."

"I can't help that," said Sansotta, "you got to be moving right away."

Rico laughed.

"Don't get funny," he said.

"Don't you get funny," said Sansotta; "you ain't in no shape to get funny."

"Maybe you better call the bulls and turn me up," said Rico.

"Well," said Sansotta, "you got to be moving, that's all."

4

RICO was acutely conscious of his position. A lonely Youngstown yegg in a hostile city without friends or influence. Yeah, funny! Just a no-account yap in a burg like Hammond and not four months ago he had been a big guy in a big burg.

He put on his ulster and went out. The wind was cold and it was snowing. He walked around for a while, keeping to the dark streets, then, chilled through, he went into a little Italian restaurant for a cup of coffee and a sandwich.

The waiter, an Italian boy with a handsome dark face, brought Rico his food. When he set it down on the table he grinned and said:

"Well, happy New Year."

Rico looked up in surprise.

"Yeah," he said, "thanks."

He felt better. This anonymous friendliness cheered him up. While he was eating, he watched the Italian boy, who was wiping off the counter and singing.

"Nice kid," thought Rico.

When Rico finished his coffee, he lit a cigarette and sat smoking. He felt comfortable. Looking around the restaurant, he saw that there was a mechanical piano up front. Like Pete's!

"Say," he called, "let's have a little music."

"Sure," said the boy.

He put a slug in the piano. It played Farewell To Thee in tremolo. Rico felt sad. He called the boy back and gave him a dollar.

"Keep the change, kid," he said.

The mechanical piano stopped on a discord, and Rico got to his feet. While he was putting on his coat two men came in the front door. One of them went up to the counter and ordered a cup of coffee, but the other stopped and stood staring at Rico.

Rico, noticing the man's scrutiny, put his hand inside his coat and started out, but the man touched him on the shoulder and whispered :

"Things ain't going so good, are they, Rico?"

Rico stared at the man and demanded :

"Who the hell are you?"

Then he recognized him. It was Little Arnie's doorman, Joseph Pavlovsky, one of the guys he had chased.

"I'm one of Arnie's boys," said Pavlovsky; "I been in Hammond ever since you gave us the rush."

"Yeah?" said Rico.

"Straight," said Pavlovsky. "I been in the beer racket over here and I cleaned up. I'm going back to the big burg next month."

Rico envied him.

"Yeah?" said Rico.

"You sure pulled one on 'em, Rico," said Pavlovsky; "you always was a smart boy, Rico."

"Aw, can that," said Rico, and, pulling away from Pavlovsky, he went out.

The wind was blowing hard now and it had stopped snowing. Rico turned up his coat collar and started toward Sansotta's. But he hadn't gone half a block when he realized that he was being followed. He turned just in time to see two men pass under an archlight.

"It's Little Arnie's boy," he said, "looking for seven grand."

Rico took out his gun, got behind a telephone pole and fired a warning shot. The two men ran for cover and Rico ducked down an alley, ran for two blocks, then turned up another alley and doubled back. He had lost them.

When the look-out let him in he said :

"Louis, the boss wants to see you."

Rico went up to Sansotta's room.

"Well?" he said to Sansotta.

"Cesare," said Sansotta, "a friend of mine is pulling out for Toledo tomorrow night. He'll take you for fifty bucks."

"What's his game?"

"Running dope."

"It's O.K. with me," said Rico.

Rico went up to his room, took off his overcoat, and flung himself down on the bed. He'd have to pull out now whether he wanted to or not.

5

THE dope-runner dropped Rico at the edge of town. It was about five o'clock in the morning and still dark. A heavy fog had come in from Lake Erie and a damp, cold wind was blowing. Rico walked up and down to keep warm while waiting for a car. He felt pretty low.

"Yeah," said Rico, "right back where I started from."

The headlight on the street-car cut through the fog. The motorman didn't see Rico and ran past him.

"Ain't that a break?" said Rico.

There wouldn't be another car for half an hour. Rico decided to walk. He turned up his coat collar against the damp wind and lit a cigar. His mind was full of resentment. Yeah, by God, a lousy street-car wouldn't even stop for him.

Rico got a room at a bachelor's hotel on the waterfront, and went to bed. It was about five o'clock in the evening when he woke up. He doused his face at the washstand, put on his overcoat, and went out.

He ate at a little Italian restaurant where he and Otero used to split a bowl of soup when things were going bad. But the place had changed. New management, new waiters, new everything. Toledo seemed small and dingy and quiet to Rico. He was a little bit puzzled.

"Didn't used to be like this," he said.

As soon as he finished his meal he walked over to Chiggi's, which was about two blocks away. But the place was dark and when Rico went up to the door to peer in he saw that it had been padlocked by the Federal Authorities.

"Ain't that a break?" he said.

He had no place to go.

There was a fruit store next to Chiggi's and Rico went in. A little Italian girl came to wait on him.

"Listen, sister," said Rico, "you know where Chiggi is now?"

"I get my grandfather," she said.

She went into the back of the store and returned with an old Italian who had crinkly grey hair and wore earrings.

"Listen, mister," said Rico, "could you tell me where Chiggi is now?"

The old man just looked at him. Rico felt a little uneasy.

"No speak English?" he asked.

"Yes," said the old man, "I speak good English. What do you want with Chiggi?"

"Well," said Rico, "Chiggi used to be a pal of mine, but I been away for three or four years and now I don't know where to find him."

"Chiggi has had trouble," said the old man; "he is in the prison."

"Yeah?" said Rico. "Atlanta hunk?"

"Yes," said the old man, "Chiggi is in Atlanta. It is too bad. Chiggi was good to the poor. When my wife was sick and my business was not going good, Chiggi gave me money."

"Yeah," said Rico. "Chiggi staked me too."

Rico took out a cigar and gave it to the old man.

"Listen," he went on, "do you know where any of Chiggi's old bunch is?"

"Yes," said the old man, "Chiggi's boy has got a place a couple of blocks from here."

The old man wrote down the address for Rico.

Young Chiggi was a dressed-up wop and thought he was a lot better than his father. He wouldn't even wait on a customer but sat all day in the back of his joint reading the *Police Gazette* or playing solitaire. Things were breaking good for Young Chiggi and he was thinking about selling out and going to Chicago or Detroit.

He had been in the beer and alcohol racket for over three years, first with his father, then by himself, and now with Bill Hackett, known as Chicago Red. He bought diamonds and automobiles and he kept his woman in a big apartment.

When Rico was shown into his office by one of his bartenders, he didn't even look up but went on with his game of solitaire. The bartender went out and Rico sat down across from Young Chiggi.

"Chiggi," said Rico, "I want to talk to you a minute."

Chiggi didn't look up.

"All right," he said.

"Listen," said Rico, "put them cards down. I want to talk business."

Chiggi looked up and stared at Rico.

"Say," he said, "where the hell do you get that stuff! I don't know you."

"Your old man was a pal of mine," said Rico.

"Well, Buddy," said Chiggi, "that don't help you none with me, 'cause me and the old man had a split-up. He thought he was so damn wise, see, but they got him behind the bars and I'm running loose."

"Yeah?" said Rico, "well, that's a tough break for the old man. You see, your old man staked me once and I thought I'd look him up and get even. I'm pretty well heeled right now and I'm looking for a place to lay in."

Chiggi looked at Rico with interest.

"Looking for a place to lay in, hunh? Bulls after you?"

"Yeah," said Rico.

Chiggi put his cards away. Then he took out a couple of cigars and offered Rico one. They sat smoking.

"Well," said Chiggi, "maybe I can take care of you."

"That's the talk," said Rico; "got some rooms up above?"

"No," said Chiggi, "but a friend of mine's got a boarding house next door that's O.K. Now about that jack the old man staked you to, you can give it to me, 'cause he owes me plenty."

Rico said nothing, but took out his fold and counted out a hundred and fifty dollars. He knew he had to buy his way in.

Rico selected his room carefully. It was on the side of the house and could not be reached from the outside as there were no porches near it. It had two doors, one opening into the front hall, one into the back hall. The doors themselves were heavy and could be barred from the inside. It was a good hide-out.

Rico's plans were vague. He had plenty of money and if he went easy with it he would be able to live a year or more in comparative comfort. But Rico could not bear the thought of a year of inactivity. What would he do with himself? He had no vices. He couldn't amuse himself by getting drunk, or taking dope, or playing faro. He didn't mind losing a couple hundred dollars gambling occasionally, but you can't put in a whole year gambling. He thought if things went right that maybe he'd move on to New York, but that would be risky and one slip and he was gone. No, he didn't see much ahead of him.

Rico spent most of the day in his room, lying on the bed reading, or else going over and over in his mind the episodes leading to his rise and fall. The resentment he had been experiencing ever since he got to Hammond had grown till it had became almost an obsession. He was never in a good humour. When he was not reading or thinking about Chicago he would pace up and down his room and wait for night. He got so, finally, that he could sleep twelve hours every day and this helped some.

At night he would go down to Chiggi's and play pool or shoot crap. Sometimes there would be a big poker game and he would sit in. He was known as Youngstown Louis and nobody in the place had the slightest idea who he really was.

Everything was against Rico. The very virtues that had been responsible for his rise were liabilities in his present situation. He had no outlet for his energy; the self-discipline which had marked him out from his fellows was of no use to him here; and the tenacity of purpose that had kept him at high tension while he was the Vettori gang chief had no object to expend itself on.

"I am nobody, nobody," Rico would say.

Sometimes at night he would go to one of the call-houses on a nearby street and spend a couple of hours with one of the women. But he got very little pleasure from these infrequent debauches. He used to wonder what had happened to the blonde he had spent old Chiggi's stake on, and was positive that if he could find her it would do him a lot of good, but she had disappeared and nobody had any idea where she had gone.

Rico tried to buy his way in. Chiggi was agreeable but Chicago Red was not. Chicago Red had taken a dislike to Rico from the first and never missed an opportunity of bullying him. Chicago Red had left Chicago under a cloud. There was a rumour that he had got in bad with a South Side gang over there and had left to keep from getting bumped off. Red was over six feet tall and weighed about two hundred pounds; he had muscles like a wrestler, a bull neck, and enormous hairy hands.

Rico kept away from him as much as possible to avoid trouble. But Red seemed to take a delight in worrying Rico, probably because, despite the fact that Rico never argued with him, always let him have his way, he felt that Rico was not impressed.

One night there was a big poker game going on in Chiggi's back room. Rico was winning. About midnight Red came in and wanted to sit in, but there was no place for him.

"Louis," he said, "get the hell off that chair and let a man get in the game."

"Not a chance," said Rico.

"Listen, Dago . . ." said Red.

"Don't call me Dago," said Rico, looking hard at Red.

"Get off that chair or I'll throw you off," said Red starting towards Rico.

But Chiggi grabbed Red from behind and pulled him into the next room.

When the game broke up, Chiggi came in and said to Rico:

"When you get settled up, come in the office."

After the other players had gone Rico went into Chiggi's office. Red was sitting with his feet on the desk and Chiggi was walking up and down.

"Well, Dago," said Red, "did you clean 'em?"

"Yeah," said Rico.

"Sit down, Louis," said Chiggi; "we want to talk to you."

Rico sat down.

"Louis," said Chiggi, "I don't know whether you're wised up or not, but we have been hitting the rocks. The bulls got two of our men and a big load of alcohol, and a couple of days ago another one of our carts got hijacked at Monroe. See, so we're pretty low."

"Yeah?" said Rico.

"Well," said Chiggi, "we want a stake, don't we, Red?"

"Yeah," said Red, "and we ain't any too particular where we get it."

"Well," said Rico, getting up, "you got a lot of guys around here. Ask them."

"Listen, Red," said Chiggi, "you keep your goddamn lip out of this."

Red got to his feet suddenly and stood glaring at Chiggi.

"Why, you lousy small-time wop, I guess you don't know who you're talking to, do you?" He raised his arm and pointed at Rico. "You see that guy there, he thinks he's the best there is, got it? He thinks he's the biggest dago outside of Italy, and here you go honeying after him like we couldn't get a stake no place else. But I ain't begging no goddamn dago to stake me."

Chiggi looked helplessly at Rico.

"Yeah," said Red, "and while we're talking, I'm getting sick of the way that bird there sits around and don't say nothing and acts like he was God-only-knows-who. Yeah, I'm getting good and sick of it, Chiggi."

"Well," said Chiggi, "when you get real sick of it, why beat it."

Red laughed.

"Gonna stick to your dago buddy, are you? Well, he's got the jack. But what're you gonna do when you need a guy that's got the guts?"

This was too much for Rico. He said:

"What do you know about guts? I guess you ain't so tough or they wouldn't have run you out of Chi."

"Will you listen to that!" said Red; "all right, buddy, you said your piece and you sure spoke out of turn. Why, dago, where I come from you wouldn't live five minutes. Now I'm gonna show you how they treat smart dagos in Chi."

Red made a motion toward his coat pocket, but Rico beat him to it. He pulled his gun from the holster under his armpit and covered Red.

"Red," he said, "in Chicago I wouldn't let you rob filling-stations for me."

Red stood with his hands up, looking from Rico to Chiggi.

"Don't bump him off, Louis," said Chiggi.

"I wouldn't waste a bullet on him," said Rico; then glaring at Red he went on: "You been getting away with this rough stuff too long, Red. I'm Cesare Bandello!"

Red's mouth fell open and he stood staring at Rico. Chiggi took Rico by the arm.

"Are you Rico?" he cried.

Rico nodded and put up his gun. Red dropped his hands, sank into a chair and wiped the sweat from his face.

"You sit down, Chiggi," said Rico, "and I'll do the talking."

Chiggi sat down.

"Lord," said Red, "so you're Rico? Steve Gollancz told me you was a big fellow."

"Steve never seen me," said Rico.

Chiggi leaned forward eagerly.

"You gonna put in with us, Louis?"

Rico said:

"I'll put in a third, but I got to boss the works or I won't put in nothing."

Chiggi looked at Red.

"That's O.K. with me," said Red.

Chiggi got to his feet and danced a few steps.

"Hurray for us," he cried.

6

UNDER Rico's guidance Chiggi's gang prospered. Chicago Red, impressed by Rico's reputation, carried out his orders and never argued; Chiggi also. And Chiggi's men were influenced by the attitude of their former bosses. Rico made decisions quickly, seldom asked for advice, and was nearly always right. Chiggi and Red were used to doing things on a small scale and hated to split with the authorities, but Rico had been in the game long enough to know that to make money you've got to spend money. Through Antonio Rizzio, one of Old Chiggi's friends, now a minor politician, Rico got in touch with some of the high-ups and bought protection. Chiggi's alcohol runners were no longer picked up and in a little while Chiggi's business had doubled. But, due to this increase in business, a new difficulty had arisen; hijackers. They waylaid Chiggi's men and robbed them of their cargoes. There was a well-organized gang of them around Monroe, Michigan, and they began to cut into Chiggi's profits. Rico tried rerouting his runners and this was successful for a month or two, but the Monroe gang soon got on to it, and the trouble started over again. Rico took a chance. He ordered three sho-sho guns from a firm in Chicago. These small automatic rifles, as formidable as machine-guns, were concealed in special cases under the seats of the trucks. Rico instructed his runners in the use of them and after a few encounters the Monroe gang decided that it would be more lucrative and also safer to confine their hijacking to smaller bootleggers who were not equipped with artillery.

Rico was pleased with his success, but hardly satisfied. This was small stuff and, as he could take no active part in it, he had a good deal of time on his hands. Of course he was a pretty big guy for Toledo and around Chiggi's he was king, but, after all, Chiggi's boys were a mighty poor lot, worse even than Little Arnie's, and their adulation wasn't worth much.

But that wasn't the worst of it. Rico knew that he had blundered badly in revealing his identity to Chiggi and Chicago Red. Neither of them was very dependable. Chiggi talked incessantly, contradicting himself, forgetting what he had said two minutes after he had said it; and all this talk was directed at one object: self-glorification. An association with Cesare Bandello, of Chicago, was something to brag about and Rico knew it. Chicago Red as a rule was not very talkative, but when he got drunk he would boast about his former connection with Steve Gollancz. Rico feared them both. Sometimes when the three of them were alone together he would caution them. There was only one thing that reassured Rico. Chiggi's prosperity depended on him, and Rico knew that both Chicago Red and Chiggi were aware of it.

At about seven o'clock one night Rico went out for supper. He ate at the little Italian restaurant where he and Otero used to split a bowl of soup when things were bad. He always sat facing the front door at the table in the back of the place. In this position he could see everyone who came in and also he could keep an eye on the people at the tables. On his right and a couple of feet ahead of him was a little window which looked out on an alley. While Rico was finishing his coffee he happened to glance at the window. When he did, a face which had been pressed against the window-pane was hastily withdrawn. Rico got up, put on his hat and paid his check.

"I'm going out the back way," he said to the counterman.

"O.K., boss."

"If anybody comes in here and asks for Louis De Angelo take a good look at him."

"All right, boss," said the counterman.

Rico went out through the kitchen door, which opened onto a little cement court where the refuse from the restaurant was dumped. The big garbage cans along the wall were in the shadow and, as Rico stepped out, a man jumped up from behind one of the cans and put a gun against him. Rico threw himself to the ground, the gun exploded harmlessly, and the man made a break for the alley, stumbling over the cans. Rico fired from a prone position and missed. Then he jumped to his feet and ran out into the alley. The man had disappeared.

"God," said Rico, "if that boy didn't almost pull one on me."

One of the cooks opened the back door and put his head out.

"What the hell!" he said.

"Damned if I know," said Rico; "a couple of guys was popping at each other out here in the alley."

"Some of them bootleggers," said the cook.

Rico took a cab back to Chiggi's. He was very much perturbed. Whoever that boy was he certainly meant business.

"Well," said Rico, "somebody has sure spilled something."

As soon as he came in Chiggi rushed up to him and grabbed him by the arm.

"Louis," he said, "Red's drunk and we can't do nothing with him."

Rico stared at Chiggi.

"Where's he been?"

"Why," said Chiggi, "he's been on a bat with some Chicago guys."

"Hell," cried Rico, "where is he?"

Chiggi led Rico back into one of the private rooms. Red was sitting at a table with a half empty quart of whiskey on the table beside him. When he saw Rico he cried :

"If it ain't old Rico himself! By God, I been drinking all day. I can hardly see but nobody can put me under the table, ain't that so, boss? Yes sir, I'd like to see the bastard that could drink Rico's buddy under the table."

Rico turned to Chiggi.

"A guy tried to pop me over at Frank's. This bird has spilled something. I got to be moving."

Chiggi's eyes got big.

"You gonna pull out, Louis?"

"I got to," said Rico; "somebody's looking for that seven grand."

"Jesus, Louis," said Chiggi, "what we gonna do without you?"

"Best you can," said Rico. "Go get me a cab, Chiggi, I'm moving right now."

Chiggi went out of the room. Rico took Red by the shoulders and shook him. Red blinked his eyes.

"Red," said Rico, "was you on a bat with some Chicago guys?"

"Was I?" cried Red; "spent a hundred bucks on them birds."

"Any of them know me?"

Red rolled his head from side to side, and sang, then he smashed his fists down on the table.

"Rico," he said, "old Red's going back to the big burg, yes sir, old Red's tired of this tank town. Old Red's got a good stake now and he's moving. They run me out once but I ain't scairt of them no more. I'm going back and show 'em who Red Hackett is. Yeah bo!"

Rico shook him.

"Listen, Red," he said, "did any of them birds know me?"

Red lolled his head, trying to focus his eyes on Rico.

"One of them guys was a personal friend of yours," said Red; "fact, he asked me if you wasn't laying up here, see, he knew all right; wasn't no harm in telling him nothing."

"Who was he?" shouted Rico.

Red thought for a moment then he said:

"I can't seem to remember. He's a wop, all right, a bald-headed wop."

"Scabby!" Rico exclaimed.

Good God, wasn't that a break! Scabby hated him and Scabby would sell his own mother out for a split on seven grand. Rico felt resentful. Just his damn luck to get mixed up with a bunch of yellow-bellies and softies.

Chiggi came in.

"Cab out in front, Louis," he said.

Rico pointed at Red.

"That guy spilled the works. For two bits I'd bump him off."

Rico was furious. He made a move toward his armpit, but one of the bartenders opened the door and yelled:

"The bulls!"

"What!" cried Rico.

The bartender was trembling all over and his face was white.

"Police car out in front, boss."

Rico made a dive for the door but Chiggi grabbed him by the arm.

"Out the back, Louis."

Chiggi leapt across the room and pulled a switch and all the lights in the place went out. Then he took Rico by the arm and led him through the hall and out into a little court at the rear.

"So long, Louis," he said.

Chiggi slammed the door. Rico was in utter darkness.

"A hell of a chance I got," he said.

He stepped cautiously out into the alley back of the court and took a look around. The alley was blind to his right; to his left it came out onto a main thoroughfare and there was a bright arc light at the end. Rico took out his gun and moved slowly toward the arc light.

"You can't never tell," he said; then, in an excess of rage: "They'll never put no cuffs on this baby."

When he was within fifty feet of the main thoroughfare a man appeared at the end of the alley way, a big man in a derby hat. He saw Rico and immediately blew a blast on his whistle. Rico raised his gun and pulled the trigger; it missed fire.

Rico was frantic. He wanted to live. For the first time in his life he addressed a vague power which he felt to be stronger than himself.

"Give me a break! Give me a break!" he implored.

The man in the derby hat raised his arm and Rico rushed him, pumping lead. Rico saw a long spurt of flame and then something hit him a sledge-hammer blow in the chest. He took two steps, dropped his gun, and fell flat on his face. He heard a rush of feet up the alley.

"Mother of God," he said, "is this the end of Rico?"

There is an extensive list of NO EXIT PRESS crime titles to choose from. All the books can be obtained from Oldcastle Books Ltd, 18 Coleswood Road, Harpenden, Herts AL5 1EQ by sending a cheque/P.O. (or quoting your credit card number and expiry date) for the appropriate amount + 10% as a contribution to Postage & Packing.
Alternatively, you can send for FREE details of the NO EXIT PRESS CRIME BOOK CLUB, which includes many special offers on NO EXIT PRESS titles and full information on forthcoming books. Please write clearly stating your full name and address.

NO EXIT PRESS Vintage Crime

Halo in Blood — Howard Browne £3.99 pb, £9.95 hb
Halo for Satan — Howard Browne £3.99 pb, £9.95 hb
Seven Slayers — Paul Cain £3.99 pb, £9.95 hb
Fast One — Paul Cain £4.95 pb, £9.95 hb
The Dead Don't Care — Jonathan Latimer £3.95 pb, £9.95 hb
The Lady in the Morgue — Jonathan Latimer £3.99 pb, £9.95 hb
Murder in the Madhouse — Jonathan Latimer £3.99 pb, £9.95 hb
Headed for a Hearse — Jonathan Latimer £3.99 pb, £9.95 hb
Red Gardenias — Jonathan Latimer £3.99 pb

Green Ice — Raoul Whitfield £3.99 pb, £9.95 hb
Death in a Bowl — Raoul Whitfield £3.99 pb, £9.95 hb
The Virgin Kills — Raoul Whitfield £3.99 pb, £9.95 hb

NO EXIT PRESS Contemporary Crime

Hard Trade — Arthur Lyons £2.99 pb
The Killing Floor — Arthur Lyons £2.99 pb
Day of the Ram — William Campbell Gault £2.99 pb
Three with a Bullet — Arthur Lyons £2.99 pb
Ask the Right Question — Michael Z. Lewin £2.99 pb
Out of Time — Michael Z. Lewin £2.99 pb
Castles Burning — Arthur Lyons £2.99 pb (5/89)
Dead Ringer — Arthur Lyons £2.99 pb (5/89)
Act of Fear — Michael Collins £2.99 pb (6/89)

THE LADY IN THE CAR WITH GLASSES AND A GUN — Sebastian Japrisot £2.99
Dany Longo is 26, blonde, beautiful and short-sighted. After borrowing her employer's car to drive to the south of France, she is confronted with one terrifying incident after another. She is handed the coat she forgot yesterday, the garage man checks the car he repaired the day before and a policeman asks her if she got back to Paris on time the previous night . . . when she had been there all day!
When she is attacked, her glasses smashed, her hand crushed and then she is confronted by a man in the boot of her car, Dany belives she is going mad. Japrisot brilliantly developes this into a tangled mystery story that won 'Le Prix d'Honneur' when first published.

NO EXIT CRIME CUTS brings the very best in crime writing, old and new at unbeatably low prices!

FAST ONE — Paul Cain (New Edition) £1.99

WAX APPLE — Tucker Coe (aka Donald Westlake) £1.99
Mitch Tobin, ex NYPD policeman was sacked for neglect that resulted in the death of his partner and friend. Racked by guilt, Tobin retires into a grim artificial world of his own until he is drawn out to investigate a series of suspicious fatal accidents at the Midway sanatorium. Five minutes after arriving Tobin is a victim himself, left with a broken arm, a headache and no idea where to begin. Then the fire escape collapses and the dirty game becomes murder!

LITTLE CAESAR — W. R. Burnett £1.99
CHICAGO. Girls and pimps, bootleggers and booze, killers and 'typewriters'. Go down the mean dark streets and see the cats sniffing the corpes. Go down the alleys and meet Rico, and Otero, Bat Carillo and Baa Baa Otavio, Killer Pepi and Kidney Bean. There are the squirrels, flapping to stay alive – Blondy Belle and Seal-Skin, Blue Jay and Olga. All playing for power. All certain to die! Little Caesar is the prototype underworld novel that inspired a whole generation of gangster films.

BURGLARS CAN'T BE CHOOSERS — Lawrence Block £1.99
Introducing Bernie Rhodenbarr, New York City's prince of thieves – who really should have known better!
When the mysterious pear-shaped man with a lot of uncomfortably accurate information about Bernie and his career offered him 5 big ones to liberate a blue leather box – unopened – it would have been a good time to plead a previous engagement, but times were tough. Everything was straightforward until two men in blue coats arrived before the liberation. Still all was not lost, there was always a way to work things out – but then they discover the body in the bedroom!

BOOK
TOKEN